by Eve Shelnutt:

The Love Child (1979)
The Formal Voice (1982)
The Musician (1987)

THE MUSICIAN

EVE SHELNUTT

BLACK SPARROW PRESS SANTA ROSA 1987

THE MUSICIAN. Copyright © 1987 by Eve Shelnutt.

Some of these stories have appeared in the following publications: *The Alabama Literary Review; An American Christmas,* Peachtree Publishers, Atlanta; *Apalachee Quarterly; Beloit Fiction Journal; Chariton Review; Clockwatch Review; Cream City Review; Epoch; From Mt. San Angelo; Greensboro Review; Ohio Review; Perigraph; Sun Dog; Three Rivers Poetry Journal;* and *Western Humanities Review.*

Library of Congress Cataloging-in-Publication Data

Shelnutt, Eve, 1943–
  The musician.

  I. Title.
PS3569.H39363M8   1987   813'.54   87-11764
ISBN 0-87685-699-7
ISBN 0-87685-698-9 (pbk.)
ISBN 0-87685-700-4 (signed ed.)

to Mark Shelton

and

to my son

Greg Shelnutt

"The house was quiet because it had to be.
The quiet was part of the meaning . . ."

Wallace Stevens

Contents

THE MUSICIAN

Angelus

Luke 1: 26-38

When Momma died, we moved like cows at twilight, her body a salt lick. When we leaned close, our neck bells clanged—Claire, Josie, me (the white-faced one) ready to be stripped clean, a puny minister's words like slaps on our flanks, and "Shall We Gather at the River" meant to prod us back to far pasture. Afterwards, the endowed moon would no doubt shine, perfectly placed on God's right side; stars would glisten on the sky's cheek. We think, when we need to, the world colludes with us.

So, down to the sweet potato pies on the sideboard, I was sick. In my mouth sat a wad of clover, no matter the reassuring minister had left on her bureau a Bible with her dates complete. I whispered to Richard, "Only a *little's* changed," hope chewing, a habit.

And, setting the Coleman on the steps, Richard held me around the shoulders with his one good arm, rubbed my head until my high heels stopped their clicking on the stone.

For a minute I listened to the frogs move through the grass toward their burled partners, sex flaring their throats. And Richard tried—he slid his hand inside my blouse, almost assumed we could make of our bed a cropped hillside, hooves digging in, or a lily pad, my legs scissoring.

I did smile, saw for an instant how an Adam's apple also balloons. Richard's body, on other nights, was loam and, sometimes, we had annealed, rising to ride the sky, a single dipper outlined in light.

But inside the house, Nathan cried and, on that night of Momma's only real pastoral, the last sound I remember was of the screen door slamming behind me. I imagine now that Richard stood for a

13

long time, his right arm held shoulder-high and the arm warm—
because he loved me. Richard: quiet, always, the smallest gesture
filled with meaning, before *or* after its occurrence.

He said later that I had carried Nathan to the rocking chair and
through the night had rocked, a rowing, I thought when he told me.
And if that is so, Momma did not budge that night, not even to
Nathan's sweet-smelling breath, enough going in and out to part
water for her passage through, had I been prepared.

In the South, for death and malingering, everyone brings food.
Otherwise, my sisters are useless, Josie, for instance, so rich I have
thought, since she came into it, of money as quilted, adorning like
Japanese jackets cropped at the girls' waists and buttoned to the
vulnerable throats. And if Ralph made it in the car parts business,
Josie had wit sufficient to read *Architectural Digest,* fix them up a
place so that from whence it came wouldn't seep—bolstered head-
boards, etcetera. She sings even in her sleep.

And Claire loves men above all, so, sensing time, the body's slip-
page, she mentions now and then joining the Peace Corps, in,
preferably, she adds, a hot climate, and we think: lower standards; or
where, I think, the blood's temperature rises, an equalizer, her life's
rage culled to her most-used phrase, "Daddy was pure-tee shit." I expect one day to get a letter from Bolivia, and Josie, who has learned
how to talk from watching T.V. interview shows, will say, "Well,
she's comfortable with it; all we can do is be as caring by mail as we
can be." So they are useless as cudweed or rocks in a well. Momma,
after Daddy left us, more or less gave up on us, which is to say she
was, even wild and ravaged at the end, mostly accurate.

The next day, wearing tennis shoes for their quiet, I paced the
tiny house, holding Nathan against my chest. Nathan, who is not
mine and Richard's but Poppa's and his last wife's boy, loaned me for
his safekeeping when Libby refused to believe he'd died on her. She
went, I think, looking for Poppa, in roadside bars, T.V. stations, used

14

car lots, the places where in this civilized world anything can happen, such as her meeting him over the hood of a Packard—himself gleaming and far enough away, I expect, she couldn't count his teeth.

Of course I accepted Nathan, breathing not a cautionary word as she popped her gum, waving, saying, "Ya'll be good, you hear?" And as she drove out of sight, I concentrated on Nathan's silk pulse throbbing at the crown of his head. How much did Momma know? That first day I had placed him on the bed at her feet, his tiny and hot, hers cooling.

I walked our rooms; again I held one hand on Nathan's head.

At noon, Richard made his sandwiches on his own, even cleaned the counter, the mayonnaise knife, his milk glass, when, but out of respect for me, he would have heated up Josie's casserole of tuna fish and mushroom soup.

But I don't think his menu lacked variety. Later, under the front car seat, on the driver's side, I found two empty Vienna sausage cans, the pulled-off lids curved neatly inside them and, crushed into one, a waxed paper wrapper emptied of saltines. I think he ate them on that day. It was mid-August, hottest month. Did he eat in the car with the windows rolled, the sausages' congealed juice dripping in the car's heat, or, if he rolled the windows down, did gnats flit at his eyes? We see, I think now, so little of how another shares our grief.

Those stuck hours of Momma's, Nathan's breathing was itself a bell against my knotted chest, and we moved through time rhythmically, against which the measured thought cannot compete, and so I barely noticed Richard. I remember, though Nathan never will, we stopped in the evening to stoop by Momma's bed, smootheddown. I pulled from beneath it her box of mementos, and for a time we sat beside it, Nathan on my crossed legs as I leafed through—all of Poppa's letters, bits of ribbon, lists of presents to give or given, a diary with seven entries which began, "Today . . ."

Lifting Nathan, I went to the back door to stand watching Richard clean out the well, one sandy bucketful after another slopping over his shoulder onto the red clay behind him where, with each bucketful, the gully roiled. Given his one good arm, the other, he claimed, lost at the elbow one evening at the saw mill while daydreaming of meeting me—given what, mere absence?—it was a ballet of sorts Richard performed, when the graceless body compensates.

I remember thinking as I watched, If I were to leave you, what of the arm would you tell the girl next in line? And I thought for a minute that I could hear Richard whisper in his night-time voice as she, too, protested, "Well, it's still *gone*," and then his laughing. So he would entice her too by what he couldn't prove, the only, I'd say now, really plausible enticement.

That second night after Momma's lowering-down, I dreamed and woke from dreaming to go sit again by Momma's box, fingering this and that as I listened to Richard and Nathan move in the bed and crib, and to the sound of the backyard pine brushing against the screen. When a wind riffled the trees, I could hear, too, the well's chain scraping the wooden lid, and cicadas calling one another across the field. Dear Claire and Josie, I wanted to ask, do you ever hold still for a minute and *listen*, Momma's oars, for instance, sucking at the water's edge? *Don't cry, Nathan*, I whispered, *above all now*.

It was then, I think, that I happened to remember Calvin. And where were *his* remembrances, the miniature box he gave her, with its medallion and, inside, the tiny heart on a chain, with his name and date? When he courted Momma, he brought his sheet music, singing bass, and her, soprano, unaccompanied, because Claire wheezed with pneumonia. She couldn't, she said, play a thing, and lay like a flower atop the covers, June through August. So, to their a cappella, she caught her breath, fever hovering at 101, Momma, *I* hoped, in love.

Calvin was fat, he sunk the sofa in, and had been fat for so long his suits fit.

"I hate him," said Claire in the bedroom with her magazines and the flute case lying open in which she kept her nail polishes. "So you two find a way to get rid of him." She sat up then. "I hate, of course,

16

our father worse, but that, now, is beside the point. Get me some water, and for God's sakes wash your hair. Can't anybody but me keep appearances up?" This even with her hair stringy, the doctor on his house calls saying she *could* get up and walk around. "Where to?" she'd ask.

And on that day of Momma's being held to shore, I wanted to know *when* Claire had learned the old-fashioned power of staying put.

Claire painted her nails, looked at them, wiped the polish off, painted them another color, the hand asking for the water never the same as took it. Claire was so subtle we loved her as we sneered.

Calvin proposed to Momma in graceful time, and, for a time, Momma wore his ring. "I'm seeing," she said, and for days Josie and I imagined a house in Anderson with fixed screens and two flushing toilets. Since he directed the choir, we would have to wear hats, and, from the pews, we imagined, we would watch Momma sing again in public, her face beatific in the eleven o'clock light.

"And what would *I* do?" asked Claire. "*Think* on it," because she was the oldest and knew in exactitude what she meant when she said, at 10:00 each Sunday night, "He'd better *not* stay."

"You won't *always* be sick."

"I will," she said, "always and forever."

Hopping around of the gravel drive by his Chevy, Josie and I leaned our heads into his window and we told him, "Momma still loves our Daddy." We whispered, *I* whispered, Josie sucking a finger and nodding, "More than *anything*."

Then Claire was well, Calvin's sheet music bit by bit having slipped from the coffee table, and, in a fit of progressiveness, Momma had a man come to retie the sofa springs. It turned out he tuned pianos, too, and Claire played Rachmaninoff, Momma's least-favorite, to wave Calvin out of sight—postlude.

Momma should have kept his little box and miniature heart on the filigree chain. And did he ever diet? Sitting on the linoleum by Momma's box, I envisioned him as shrunken, his back, as he conducted the black-robed choir in Anderson, thin as a beetle's, arms waving like little legs when the body's overturned. I missed him; I thought I missed him for Momma's sake.

I remember that, after we had whispered the evening truth to Calvin, I made Josie clean out our fort; I had her tie twigs together for a broom while I ran across the road to tell Joe, age fifteen and worldly, what we had said to Calvin. Tending his rabbits in their moonlit cages, Joe listened, said when I finished, "He'll be back—grown men are stickers," forgetting Poppa and thereby me. So I kissed him on the mouth until his breath heaved. I left him like that—full-blown—ran, laughing, and got Josie from the fort. We slammed the door, broke into Momma's innocent humming. Which is to say Momma may have been right to throw up her hands when it came to us, but wrong, wrong, wrong to say when anyone asked, "Well, I *read* to them, so no one can say I didn't try." Words, Momma, eat like sulphur, come out rolled around the motorized tongue, and your children didn't know what to do with the power. I think now that when we talk, we aren't meant to remember our tongues, how, stretched out, their muscles, oars through water, pull our hearts.

"I want you to drive us to Anderson," I told Richard, having dressed Nathan in the morning in his best diaper top. "Just drop us off in town—I want to walk around." And in the car ("We'll be fine.") I saw again how smoothly Richard drove with just one arm. I recall thinking how long it takes for expertise, especially the pinning with one hand the safety pin that held up the flapping sleeve.

And was it, that day, presentiment of my leaving him that made me wave him away, suspicion like the "o" in *forever*? I think he went to the library to read Momma's farewell in the Anderson newspaper. And if he did, would he be apt to notice that it didn't mention Poppa or Calvin or the fact that she loved music? It was a notice so short it was polite, like gloves, for instance, over chewed nails.

Calvin wasn't at the church, even though it was Wednesday, when the choir, after practice, is allowed to wear shirt sleeves and sleeveless voile dresses for the service, the sins, on Wednesdays, I always thought, not yet having had time to impact, as they say. A dallying day.

18

So Nathan and I reposed at the back pews, waiting. I must have thought Calvin would come rushing through, sheet music under one arm, his robe flapping. Mary shone from the vestibule window and, so far apart from her, Joseph, in the second window from the back, pulled his donkey and looked downward.

For a time, Nathan and I dozed, his little body stretched out flat on the maroon cushions of the pew, pure white against the deepest red, and the pew row-boat long, wood sturdy for the longest trip. Oh we had hope.

I think, now, it is time to mention other children—Ralph's and Josie's first because they have been, with such wealth, sent out into the world like miniature emissaries, or tiny travel agents advertising a place so exotic most of us will never get there. She keeps them protected through modern inventions from all ugliness, so of course they did not see Momma, not having been born, and they haven't seen Claire of late, who has yet to make it to Bolivia but is inching closer. If any of their little friends move out of town, Josie flies her children to them for a visit, any town, even foreign. And when there is a crisis on T.V., they sail Ralph's boat out into the Gulf until it blows over. I don't think she reads to them.

I didn't marry Richard. I took Nathan and found a man as good as Richard, named Quentin. He has a boy he's never seen, and our house is beautiful too, like pages from a magazine printed long ago. Nathan's grown now, also sent out, moneyless, but his brain flares with everything Momma knew. Though it may be a sin, when Nathan brings home his girls, I imagine they look like Poppa's little girls, those many, many (Momma) I am sure he scattered from Ventura to Orlando, it being simply chance we got Nathan, timing being everything.

Sometimes Quentin and I stop mid-sentence when we hear on T.V. of the child left at the hospital steps. Do we linger over the same pictures in magazines—the children from Venezuela or Peru who haven't eaten in months? One day we may ask for one ourselves, a girl I would name Libby after Poppa's last wife.

Claire had a little boy, Ben, who called one day to say Claire was getting strange. By phone, we arranged his living with Josie and Ralph, learning to sail a boat and how to like fine food, and Claire rarely sees him. On the phone Claire is wistful, and it has never, I am sure, crossed her mind to ask when Little Ben might ask about *his* Poppa. And so, in her stead, I imagine Ben's daddy in Savannah, not far from Josie, tending boats off-shore. And, of course, his other wife has their two children, and *her* two, plus cousins on visits, all learning to fish, tie knots, unfurl.

Of course, too, Calvin never came to the church. We found him, at 4:00 in the afternoon, in the Pinehall Rest Home, off Interstate 29. We went by taxi, the driver telling me, "Fine boy you got there," and I held Nathan closer, forgetting, as we got out, his bag of food, milk, the clean shirt. So, until the driver noticed, everyone who rode with him that afternoon saw reminders of Nathan, all white, and the green of his jar of spinach, color of leaves.

And Calvin was thin; he was beetle-like, although his arms could not lift. "Just a goodwill visit," I told the nurse, who cooed over Nathan. And so we sat by Calvin. I wanted to hum his favorite hymn. I wanted to sing Momma's favorite song, my voice so like hers he would think she was in his room. "Hi, Girlie," he whispered, then fell asleep again.

So we sat, me looking at the pictures on his bedside table as Nathan squirmed—four children, grown, and the woman standing behind them as pretty as Momma in her prime, their house no doubt beautiful, scrubbed clean.

I placed Nathan by his cooling feet; I let Nathan nap there. And if I did not imagine I saw Calvin smile, it was because, I think, I didn't need to, watching Nathan's even breathing. There must have been other men Momma knew. I like to think Nathan rowed for all of them.

I called the library, Richard came for us, and, on the way home, we passed the church again. I looked at the stained glass window of

Mary as the light changed. She's stayed in my mind all this time, especially when I think, daily, of Quentin's unseen boy, or Little Ben, whom we haven't seen in a long, long time.

Even, I will not be sad if Claire calls from Bolivia, saying she's feeling better. Or sad when she sends a photograph, herself fat, as she's become, on a beach, and, behind her, in the distance, anyone's children stooping with buckets and shovels on the sandy hill.

I think now that Momma, who loved Poppa equitably well, was not discreet. I think she was polite, like Mary. Gabriel had, after all, come so far to announce that she would (except abstractly) be lonely, which Mary knew, as all women know, the ringing bells a gift from her for weary Gabriel.

Questions of Travel

Suppose," said Anna's mother, a shudder running across her chest, "he comes while I'm ironing?"

Irene's right hand would lift from the little pink dress Anna might have worn, for this had happened many times, and she would look, puzzled now, at the damp and dry spots, like a leopard's skin, Irene would think, and rub her eyes with her still-warm right hand, as if to erase thoughtlessness.

She would fold up the wooden board with its scorched cover of sheeting, smooth down the damped clothes bunched in the basket — hands the wings of butterflies, *if* her life would flower: produce Anna beside her in starched linens, with sailor's collars, and, on her, a rosebud mouth, willful limbs falling this way and that until, finally, love made her still, to be sipped.

Instead, Anna wore the wrinkled red and navy plaid or red and brown plaid or the dress of muted flowers. These clothes hung limply against Anna's thin legs, and Anna moved as if asleep. A sleepwalker, thought Irene. So there was no need to iron, now was there?

Irene hurried to put the ironing board away, behind the curtain in the hall. "Well!" she exclaimed as she pulled the girl beside her on the couch — the girl who wasn't truly her own yet — a mistake recurring until Anna smiled, claiming her section of — what? — the world? If it unfolded like a warm bolt of cloth, surely it was for Anna.

"Tell me about your day at school."

But they both were listening now, as if he *were* coming. The girl had learned, too, to tilt her head to one side, as if to hear, inconclusively, car tires whipping the wind between stands of trees, then routing the gravel outside. It was, Irene seemed to say, when, like this, she stopped abruptly an activity, simply a matter of sitting properly upright, hands folded in their laps, and allowing their mouths to form the rounded shapes from which issued the lovely words: *orchestra, oven, ostentatious* — Irene laughing at their game, which had begun, oh, when?

Then, lapsing, Irene said as she looked out the window, her fingers sliding over Anna's, "Old, old, old."

You could hear, then, a shoe hitting on a wooden floor.

So Irene laughed again, amending: "Old me," as if a finger burrowed playfully into a furry chest. "I haven't fed you yet, have I?"

Then the two would go into the tiny kitchen where Irene had nonetheless wedged a table, covered in blue chambray, with perfect triangles of yellow rickrack decorating the corners. "Sit!" Irene said. "Take a load off your feet," as if Anna were he, the awaited one. And Anna sat as Irene twirled the lazy susan cupboard beside the stove, saying, "Let's see, let's see."

Soon blue bowls with handles appeared on the table, filled with potato soup, cheese bubbling on top, and Irene smiling as Anna told about her day, which, outside, was moving from dark blue to black.

"A boy?" asked Irene. "Is there always a boy in your stories?", which puzzled Anna — what did she mean, when it was only Ralph or Jimmie, who sat near her in school?

"Well, eat up," said Irene. "God knows you'll need it," which she'd not meant to say — a muscle loosening. She felt her ribs, *his* touch against them, a finger, as if to separate them — he might enter her there — how he chose the delicate methods of preparing her, until he forgot, his body interceding. Then he was a dozen horses running through a field.

A light hung over the table where it shone brightly on their two dark heads and cast shadows on the checkered linoleum behind them. A wedge of light lit the knotted oak growing close to the tiny room which served as their kitchen. Otherwise the house was dark, even the front porch, where Irene might have left a light burning.

But of course he did not come, not that day nor the next, nor had he been to visit for months. That he *might* come was the habit, like a fish's gills opening, which meant, as if it were the proper environment, saline enough, Irene washed half of their car, ironed a portion of the clothes, let bread rise and harden until she found it cemented to a bowl.

"Old, old, old. . . ."

What Irene did when she taught at school, Anna had no way of knowing. Halfway through a song—"Row, row, row your . . ."—did Irene drift off while the children's mouths drooped and the walls of the music room became discordant? Anna did not take Irene's classes—"No need, Sugar," Irene had said, "when I can teach you myself at home," as she had intended.

But books were easier, and Anna read, sometimes humming to herself as Irene strummed the autoharp, deciding upon the next day's lessons. So words were accompanied by the chest's throbbing, and they aligned themselves into rhythmical patterns.

As a result of her reading, Anna's eyes were continually pink, a rabbit's eyes, thought Irene, and there was not so much difference between the calligraphy of grass sprouting from the ground and words from the page. "And he'll tell me to get you out into the sun."

Even there, as if the sun cut holes in the bower of leaves disproportional to her body, Anna swang in half-light. From the perspective of the tree's height, she must have appeared tiny: a miniature swing, a miniature girl swinging on it. She never tanned, even in the hottest months.

And, as it was, Irene stirred herself for school. It came, she acknowledged, with the suits she wore, not his gifts, which were for inside the house, inside their room, but suits picked out by her sister, the disgusted one who had hated him on first sight. Her duty, she said, was to keep Irene looking competent enough to return to the world, should she need to, meaning *when* she needed to, a time coming, was it not, as surely as light from stars?

Irene wore the stiff suits and her children sang on key, loudly, teeth showing, the girls' little sashes riding up around their ribs as they breathed deeply, the boys' pants dropping low. They had no hip bones, so little to cover if the pants fell. Their legs would be as white as the bellies of fish or Anna's forehead.

They loved Irene—these children—knowing nothing of what she asked when she said the words had to be rounded, that their lips should close at once when a note ended. "Not a breath after that, until I lower my arms," Irene would say. They liked her forcefulness, as if something important could issue from them. "O Mary, Mother of Jesus, O hear, O hear our cry," when this was a public school. And, for that: "O beauti-ful, for spa-cious ski-ies. . . ."

While her class sang, Anna was allowed to paint with the fifth graders, below her chronologically by a year and by many in the secret calculations Anna made of Irene's ways, one of which was that Irene was too distracted to wonder why everything Anna painted was yellow, and half-finished: suns without middles, flowers without stems, boats without sailors, shoes without feet.

"Ah! The color of music!" said Irene, pantomiming an orchestra leader and tacking Anna's picture on the refrigerator, when Anna thought of his headlights, moving through Arizona, Montana, all the states which lay hidden under her hand as she pressed it flat against her map.

Or, thought Irene, the color of breasts, mine, when he sucks them, when the stiff suits came off. In the house, she left them freed, wearing the chenille bathrobe and the fluffy slippers, no underclothes. In a dresser drawer were the white batiste nightgowns she wore afterwards, when he'd ridden her. Those she had ironed, a portion of his gifts.

Summer was over, autumn had colored the leaves before they had noticed, with light fading even as the leaves fell to allow more light. Irene called the older sister: "Buy us some of those wonderful apples you have up there. We'll come get them some Sunday." But Irene forgot, and when she wanted in the house the smell of apples, she boiled cider from the grocery, with cloves.

Anna read to the sound of Irene's playing and to the odor of autumn brought down to a kitchen pan—a bubbling of spice, which she could almost taste when she chewed the ends of her braids.

The furnace hummed—Irene ordered the oil while at school, when her other self, the one in reserve, took over. And a boy from school, who worked for Tyson's Grocery, brought the food, the list written on the back of paper printed with octaves and staves during the time Irene's students practiced inventing their own songs in the ruled books.

26

"I won't let him see you," said Irene one evening when the delivery boy came to the door just after Anna had bathed, her gown wrapped by dampness to her thin body.

"Let him see!" said Anna. "I could care less," because, to her, there was nothing to see.

"Oh no," said Irene, "no one should see you until he is *ready* to see you," which meant *he* had gotten himself ready before opening Irene's suit jacket and pulling down the straps of her slip. And, maybe, even now, he was preparing.

All that he needed stayed with him in California and, when he visited, as if it were not precious, he scattered his belongings about their room, casually. Then Irene helped him gather it all together again, place it carefully back into the leather suitcase. Anna saw from the hall—shapes, the wadded shirts, the belts hung over the chair, and shoes aligned beneath the bureau. Crossing to the bathroom, he wore a yellow towel, with his initials on it, and another like it around his neck.

Across the street, in mid-October, when all the leaves had fallen and the shack which sat behind Mrs. Rice's house became visible again, they watched a black woman move into the shack, raising the shades, swinging wide open the screen and the wooden door behind it. "Her maid," said Irene.

"*Whose* maid?"

"Mrs. Rice's! Don't you look out? Mrs. Rice used to take the car out herself, and now she has Tercell, from school, do it. She's sick, so the maid's for that."

"Oh," said Anna, and she would have forgotten, but the maid was coal-black and thin and, said Irene—young—you could tell by how she moved across the porch, sweeping it, every day, sweeping. At first, yellow leaves and the red leaves of the maples flew into the hedges. Then nothing flew, and she swept.

Tercell, the janitor from school ("*Who?*" asked Anna, to which Irene said, "Where *are* you at school? *Tercell,* who washes the black-boards," and then Anna remembered his shape engulfed in yellow dust as he slapped the erasers against the steps outside the cafeteria, face and shoulders haloed in dust), drove Mrs. Rice home from outings just as Anna and Irene drove up to their driveway after school. Turning from the car, they watched him lift her from the pillows in the back seat and carry her up the back steps, which Irene said Mrs. Rice had never sunk to using before.

Then, just as Anna and Irene had put their books down on the chair by the door, the bell began to clang in Mrs. Rice's back yard, rung by Tercell to call the black girl to her evening chores.

Irene went to the window to watch, so this became the ritual—to observe the girl tilt her head, as if the bell weren't resonating for blocks, lift the one leg swung over the arm of the chair she sat on, her black dress sliding high on her thighs as she rose with one hand at the hollow of her back. Then her right arm reached inside the screen door for the white apron, a wedge of white, a suggestion of *apron*. She tied it around her tiny waist, slapped a pocket where, Irene said, she had cigarettes. Then the slow, queenly—said Irene—descent of the steps, her head barely visible over the hedge which ran the length of the ground in front of the porch underpinnings. When her head became visible to Tercell at the bell, he let the rope go. It grew quiet again, and the last sound they heard was of the back door slamming.

"Ah so," said Irene, turning from the curtain. But what did she mean?

"Let's make some hot chocolate." But at the table Irene had nothing to say about what they had watched.

"We could go see," said Anna.

"*Us?*" said Irene. "Not us."

But Anna watched, watched as the maid came to refuse to keep her black dress on the whole afternoon and began to wear instead black tights and tight pink shorts, with high heels and yellow socks over the tights—ankle socks. But Anna was wrong, seeing less than Irene at the window. They were not tights but the girl's very skin.

"Sugar," said Irene, "you're so sweet."

Then, when Tercell rang the bell, the black girl had to enter her shack, remove the shorts and the white tee shirt, step into the black dress. She left buttoning it as she went. The bell clanged longer.

28

"She'll freeze," said Anna.

"She won't freeze," said Irene.

On a day off from school, at the Thanksgiving holiday, when Irene and Anna went to buy a turkey in case he should come, they saw Mrs. Rice in the black DeSoto, pillows surrounding her as if to hold her upright.

"She's out seeing the world for the last time," said Irene. "A month or two, a year, even, it's still the last time since she knows it."

Where, then, was the black girl? Sitting on the porch in her pink shorts, waiting. Irene saw her in her mind's eyes—it was white lace, she decided, tacked to the cuffs of her socks.

Anna tired of their watching at the window when they returned from school. The house was cold since the furnace was turned low in their absence. She wanted the warmth of the kitchen, Irene lighting the gas oven and leaving the door open as they ate their soup or chili.

Sometimes Irene brought her robe and slippers into the kitchen and changed there, before the open door of the oven. "Oh!" Irene might say, her nipples warming, standing erect.

He never wrote, had never written, so it was nothing they expected. If Anna thought of it now, it was because the black girl sometimes sat reading a letter on the porch as she waited for the bell to clang.

"What's it like where he is?" Anna asked once.

"Like here," said Irene. "Look around you!" Her right hand flung out to take in the stove, the sink, the table with the two of them sitting across from each other in the circle of light. On one wall was a calendar which the older sister had given Irene, marking the dates she would visit. "What *else*?" asked Irene.

"Why doesn't she"—Anna nodded her head as if the black girl's porch were behind their house—"sit inside, like we do?"

Irene put down her spoon on the blue cloth. She closed her eyes—considering, thought Anna. "Because, I expect," said Irene, "there's nothing *in* the house."

A bed, Irene said to herself, no one's slept in with her.

"Nothing that's hers, Sugar," which objects, Irene thought, anointed, *if* he had touched them, even a match book. *He* smoked—

Camels, so she could never pass a billboard indifferently.

"*Anointed*," said Irene, taking up their game. "Hear it?"

"Apostrophe," answered Anna, to which Irene rubbed Anna's head, saying, "You're learning something, now aren't you?"

At Thanksgiving, the maid had company, a man in a blue work shirt and two boys Anna's size, going in and out of the tiny house, slamming the screen door, positioning and repositioning the potted geraniums they had brought her. Smoke came from the chimney for the first time and, later, the boys sat on the edge of the porch, dangling their legs off the side. The door behind the screen shut and, later, when the boys began to shoot at birds with sling shots, the man opened the door and hung on a nail beside it his blue work shirt.

At the window, Irene smiled, placed her hands on her ribs, as if her fingers could fill each space. Toward twilight, the man and the two boys got into the Chevy which the man had parked on the porch beside the shack even though there was no entrance through the hedges. Wedging through, with Irene thinking she could feel the spines of the hedges brush across the tender parts of the man's skin, the three got into the tan-painted car and drove off.

"You see," asked Irene a week later, "how she leaves the extra chair on the porch?"

"*I* don't watch," said Anna. "It's you. It's not polite."

"So," answered Irene, "you're going to sound like your Aunt Alice now? Well, perhaps you don't need to watch. And I'm through now, if you want to know. I know the rest."

"Like what?" asked Anna. "You don't know."

But now the black girl could sit inside her house; eventually the bell ceased to clang; though Mrs. Rice's house was empty, smoke still came from the shack's chimney; and Irene had no lack of imagination.

In California, seen as if tiny strings had held him down, which now he broke, lumbering up so that, from the standing position, he looked normal in size, explicable, he gathered together the clothes he would need, the toiletries, the woven dolls for Anna, and perfumes, boxes of scarves and oranges. He gassed up the black car.

30

Returning once to the little house set two blocks from the ocean, he kissed once, on the thigh, the girl he was leaving behind—young and modern in her shorts, which made her body seem especially tall. He covered her to her chin with the cotton sheet. He poured bird seed into the cup of the wood cage which hung before the opened window. She was sleeping, the bird was chirping, the sun set as he drove around the corner to the ocean route.

For miles, far into the night, he would pass the billboards of elongated women pictured dressed in black velvet or the shiny fabric they called *lycra*, which made their legs look especially thin, as cave women look in primitive drawings as they walk toward the fire.

Houses shrank against the backdrop of mountains or hung precariously on the sides of hills, tree limbs dwarfing them, lifting to catch the moon's light. Stars fired the sky or neon pasted a halo against the drape of black.

In Arizona, the radio stations would fade, and silence would engulf the car. Then rain would come, a drumming, and the bodies of cave women transformed on the billboards would waver as the windshield wipers slashed across the glass. When it let up: another silence, as if all voices had stopped, as if words had not yet been invented, so women in their miniature houses, sitting straight on stools before the open fires, would appear fixed.

He would appear to Irene and Anna as huge when, at daybreak of the second day, he opened the door, coming upon them surrounded by their objects of love.

Did he think of this?

No. No, of none of it.

Disconsolate

"How cold to the living hour grief could make you!"
Eudora Welty, *"Music From Spain"*

Even from the first they could see she was martyred by it, *for having sons,* she said to herself, *one of whom they had to have.* And they would not call it a war. During the fifth week of Darrell's absence, when it was clear he would go to Korea (which had been clear to Darrell, Charlie, and Johnny all along), Irene had written to the congressman from her district to ask, "Would you tell me how many killed it would take to elevate this so-called conflict into a war? I want figures."

And the congressman had written back that she must be proud having a son in the Armed Forces (it was obvious he hadn't looked up which branch) and that the nation was eternally grateful. She tacked his letter to the wall in the kitchen—her irony, since anyone coming in would think she *was* proud. "The word *eternally* is an unfortunate choice," she would say if anyone happened to read it.

Charlie, her husband, and Johnny, the younger son, had no idea, really, of how she felt. This was clear to her when, just after Darrell was "called up," as they said, they had hired Rufus, the Negro with one arm, to help out in the dairy, which she had said was hilarious.

Looking up from their noon meal of pork chops, corn bread, green beans, and sweet milk, Charlie and Johnny had been surprised to hear that word, said dryly, the tone flat. Lately when she spoke, it was as if her lips were a pea pod unzipping to reveal pellets of words lined up separate, and with a life of their own. *Hilarious* might well have been *tragic* or *soulful,* they were so startled.

What Irene meant and could not say was that Rufus's coming to help in the place Darrell had occupied was to her like the flowing

33

together again of the Red Sea, Darrell caught and churning in salt water full of Philistines, seaweed, the spines of fish.

When she asked how Rufus could possibly milk with one arm, Charlie said, "He uses his stump, I'll call it," and he demonstrated, his elbow punching out at the air in a rhythm as his right hand squeezed. "It loosens the milk so that it flows faster," he added. "It's not only inventive, it's effective."

"I don't want to *see* it," said Irene. "Make him eat out under the trees," which was where Rufus crouched now, his plate balanced on one knee and, had she looked, his short arm jabbing out at flies or the chickens.

But, as if she *had* looked over her shoulder and through the screen, Irene said, "It's a mess," meaning the situation, when Johnny thought she meant the yard.

"We'll get to it," Johnny said, and Charlie added, "Why not help?" In his mind, he had given her special dispensation for the time being, and now he spoke to her as he would to a child he was cajoling.

"My 'war effort'?" asked Irene. She sat twirling the lazy susan of condiments in the center of the table around and around, and so that was how they left her. She heard Rufus' tin plate bang and the fork clatter in it on the stone step and, later, she stood to watch through the heat's shimmer their three forms moving across the field to the tractors.

It made her sick to pick up Rufus' plate, wiped clean with the heel of his bread, which she knew he would do no matter how much she fed him. She kept a special jelly glass full of soapy water for his forks, not knowing from where he had come, *who* he was.

Holding his plate, she shuddered at the awful intimacy of it, when she hadn't seen his face yet, and did not want to. Then looking again out the screen door, where flies buzzed around the cotton balls stuffed into the holes as if the fluff were clouds which would part to admit them, a configuration in her mind made vulnerable by Darrell's absence came to her: that Charlie and Johnny were strangers, talking to Rufus just as strangers talked to Darrell over there as they moved to the cover of an embankment. By squinting her eyes, she could see

Rufus in the middle, protected by being flanked on each side.

All afternoon, as each afternoon since she had let Darrell go, she walked through the rooms of the house where the linoleum's flowers' wilted colors lay more muted in the diffused light of the drawn shades, and the air, in deference, seemed to still itself.

The only sounds inside the house were the scuff, scuff of her house slippers and the ringing of the party line, which made her count, then say, "Ida" or "Arlene" or "Ruby."

She did not go into Darrell's room, as if now it held not death's gaping hole but a stranger's privacy, possibly with some prosthesis on the bureau, woven straps dangling by the drawer pulls and, on the nightstand, a saucer of pills, pearly-white and egg-shaped, by the glass of water with bubbles forming on the sides.

Evenings she cooked as if by rote, having now, however, to depend on Johnny to remember to bring the pail of milk to the front porch since she wouldn't go to the barn: Rufus might be jabbing the udder of the last cow or using his stump to steady the pail as he poured milk over the cooler. Charlie had not said this was how he did it, but she had imagined it, imagined even his scooping out grain with the stump while he held the bucket in one hand. Right or left— she hadn't asked, nor how it had happened.

Through the spring months she had gone often to the post office to mail packages to Darrell. Then she dressed well, as if to tell anyone who saw her how good a family Darrell came from, and so of course he would get back whole and breathing.

Because she knew it was winter there, she had sent thick wool socks and leather gloves lined with wool or rabbit's fur, and small Navy-blue knit caps which she instructed Darrell to wear under his helmet. And, by and by, he had written that he had enough socks, gloves, and couldn't wear the wool caps under his helmet, as much as he appreciated the thought. "In fact," he added, "we got a good laugh out of it—no offense," which made her feel desolate. And when finally there was nothing more to send him, she began wearing her house dresses and staying in, having bought enough air mail envelopes to last out any war.

In the beginning, too, she had stopped by Neil's Pharmacy

ostensibly to have coffee before driving back to the farm, when what she waited to do each time was say to Rita or Annie—whichever, rumpled-looking but pretty, was on duty at the time—"I got a letter from Darrell, by the way. He's fine," until out of a delicacy she hadn't thought them capable of, they said, softly, using the same words as though they had consulted one another, "We don't really know him— it was just a bunch of us going to a drive-in once in Robbie's truck."

After that, Irene had written to Darrell that she would be glad to look up any of his girls and tell them whatever he wanted. But Darrell wrote *please*, not to bother.

"Let him concentrate on his job, Momma," Johnny had said. "There'll be plenty of time for that later"—*his* view of stringency.

But: Maybe, and maybe not. It was a refrain Irene said to herself, as if her interior voice alone could keep her balanced, no matter Charlie said, "Odds are, he'll make it." And what made Charlie think the scale tilted their way?

At night, because he believed in odds and because of the pleasure of habit, Charlie reached for her, to unloosen her arms stiff at her side, to turn her head toward him from where its eyes lay staring at the ceiling—in fact, he had come to think of her in parts, which had to be coaxed from each hold as Johnny had been once at a carnival, clinging to the white horse of the carousel which had frightened him. "Oh, no," Irene would have said had she known he thought this, to assert her effacement, "it's not *me* jeopardized."

And, in the beginning, she *had* loosened easily and could be gotten into his arms, where he overlooked her stifled sobs or, as if they were water on a counter, wiped the tears off with his tee-shirt. Then, with her either laughing or crying and with him unable to tell the difference, which later he would remember, he would enter her as always and make her, he imagined, forget.

But now that she had seen Rufus walking in the protectorate of Charlie and Johnny's bodies, she felt they were people with whom she must be polite. And so now she said to Charlie, "Oh, no thank you," and turned on her side, away from him. To her he was a passenger on a bus or a transport to whom consideration must be given, meaning privacy for whatever endangerment had set him adrift.

36

"This can't go on forever," said Charlie; and she thought that he meant the war. "No," she said, "but . . . ," letting her voice trail off into the reserve in which she kept herself, when she would have said nothing of herself was there, only Darrell, and his buddies: he *had* written "we."

Them: she began, almost, to depend on them, although she had no pictures. In fact, she wouldn't permit pictures, which Darrell sent oblivious of her knowledge that, during their passage to her, anything could have happened. Johnny had them now, having gathered them up from the table when Irene had said, "Not in *my* house," slapping them down. "Darrell in uniform: what next?", when she thought at that moment she knew well what next—the visit, the letter, the flag-draped box, and finally the unadorned white cross to remind the living that the dead fell like trillium across a field.

Johnny had apparently written to Darrell of her abhorrence since he answered, "I'd send a picture of me *out* of uniform but we don't *get* out of uniform, except Chester just did because he got his toes blown off and got to wear pajamas, I expect."

So she had a name: Chester, who she imagined had by now recovered to return to Darrell's side, toes being the least extremity. Resuming her package-sending, to which Mr. Holmes at the post office said, "Well I feared you'd lost him when you didn't come in," she tucked a note in with the socks: "For Chester." As if to buy him off, for that split second when something personal between him and Darrell would matter.

And, possibly knowledgeable in a distance which by its own properties reveals what is equi-distant, Darrell did not write that Chester had enough socks, or gloves, or wool caps. Even, she thought of going into Johnny's room to look for the pictures, to glance, maybe, at Chester's face, ensconced above a uniform collar or not. He would, she thought, have one arm around Darrell, and the other friend, nameless, would be reaching across from the other side. "Three on a match," didn't they say? Then, as if to rebalance herself, she added, Three *interchangeable* on a match.

Expectation, she thought, of any kind, would kill her, and so she settled in, as she thought of it, for the ride, the destination of which was known to someone else, someone she thought of as brighter than herself.

But who? Certainly not Charlie or Johnny, their faces unassailable.

Some afternoons, when she had washed the noon dishes and wandered through the house, wishing each time that she had saved the trip to the post office until later in the day, she stood in the upstairs hall near Darrell's closed door to look at herself in the hall mirror. Was she ready—this face and body presentable enough for wherever they were headed? That she was still pretty did not matter so much as her immaculateness: order *in* the house if not outside it.

Rising one day from the table at noon, Irene went to the back screen to call, "Can't you all clean it up out there?", no matter that Charlie and Johnny sat behind her with ice tea spoons and their tall glasses of corn bread and milk. Rufus did not look up—her plight nothing to *him*, she thought, since Charlie gave the orders.

"Momma?" Johnny asked, thinking, no doubt, where would it all end. But she was watching Rufus pat the dog, with his *right* arm. So now she knew, and she hated the knowing.

When she saw Rufus one morning driving past the barn on the tractor, as if he were as capable as her husband or son, a great lassitude, like the last wind within a descending bird's wing, swept by and caught her, and set her down on the couch.

That noon she didn't begin to fix lunch until she heard Charlie and Johnny come into the house, and she had not brought in the mail. But it was bills; they looked through it as she moved around the kitchen table set in the middle of the room. She felt dizzy, and thought as she brought out leftovers from the oven, "Rufus won't like this." She opened a can of applesauce, for something new, and set it down on the table, with the withered beans and steak with gravy dried to it.

"I won't have much more of this, Irene," said Charlie.

And to that all Irene had to say was, "I won't either." A warning *or* an admission.

As they ate, she thought that if she had been a European, it would have been bred into her, how to wait in equanimity, since all foreign daughters grew upon their faces at age fifteen that look of repose, history irreplaceable and so essential it was like breath. Their bodies moved automatically with, if not hope, then the grace of knowing some inevitable truth.

38

"You have to eat," said Johnny. But Irene said, "I don't have to eat."

And that, as it turned out, was the last day Irene sent the packages to Chester, by way of Darrell.

She sat often on the couch, thinking a great lucidity had come over her. She listened to the sounds outside, especially to the voices calling back and forth to each other, even of the cows from the back pasture or the barn or the gully where the salt licks sat. She thought even of returning to church, its music, the hymns in a minor key; but the ladies, she was sure, would coo over her and make her cry or "snap out," as Charlie had begun to refer to her present way of talking.

She did not know that Charlie sometimes lifted her hands as she slept and rubbed his finger tips over her nails—bitten or torn. He thought of her during his day as sitting on the couch with her hands seemingly at rest in her lap but with her fingers pulling relentlessly and of their own volition at their own skin and nails.

And she did not know that he discussed her "state," as he called it, with Johnny and, even, with Rufus. She would have said, "Well, so what?" since how she was becoming was, he knew, to her only temporal, dismissable, a wedge of time in what for Darrell might be the limitless expanse. She would have said, "Don't concentrate on *me!*" or, simply, "Wake up!" as if she shook him, when it was Irene herself shaking in her sleep.

And she did not know that Johnny had said to Charlie, "I'm getting pretty sick of it, if you want to know," or that Charlie had answered, "I don't," *his* wife and the state of marriage which a son, present *or* absent, ought not to intrude upon.

"I want you back," he said to Irene one night, to which she said in that voice which made him cold, "I'm here, where else *am* I?"

But she was *not* there.

He thought once of asking her what she would do if Darrell *died*, but knew better than to ask, even as he imagined Johnny above them in his own room asking the same question, and answering to himself, "*I'd* get out of here."

Charlie reasoned that in such an event he would keep Rufus on and, moreover, bring Rufus's wife in to cook. Irene didn't know he *had* a wife.

To fill her days, or so she thought of it, Irene listened now to the women on the party line—not members of their church and so strangers to her, which made the eavesdropping permissible. She could picture each one—their telephone benches, picture windows, daughters who looked like them—and she came to know from listening also in the background which of them had gotten their husbands to buy a television set. She would not have had one, especially now.

Autumn was coming, which she could tell not so much from the night air in which, because Rufus had left for the day, she felt free to wander, but from the rustle of everything that had withered, and by the rasp of crickets' feet, sound cushionless now that the corn was cut.

Some evenings she took the hoe Charlie hung by the shed door and hacked at her canna lilies, looking up from them to the sky.

Inside, under the light of the lamp which hung over the center of the table, Charlie, hearing her, would look at Johnny as if to say, "She's coming out of it." And mostly he thought, since to him the latest word was the only word, "So far so good"—how, in fact, he had lived his life, of which he was proud. Secretly, he was proud of Darrell, doing what was necessary to do.

But, as if to caution himself, Charlie thought one night before going into their room how he had to censor every word he said—Johnny, too, who one day at noon had wanted to tell Irene about Rufus having played Darrell's old trick on the pick-up boys, waiting a day to put out a second time the milk they had rejected the day before for smelling of wild onion. "Wouldn't Darrell have loved it?" Johnny had said.

But when Johnny began at the table, saying, "You know what Rufus did?" Irene had raised one hand. "I don't want to *hear* about it—he's *temporary*. He'll pass right out of our lives just as quickly as he came, soon . . . ," her voice suspended because she couldn't say, too, "as Darrell gets back."

She turned then to look behind her, to Rufus sitting under the oaks. It was then, when he was alone, she hated him, the history she couldn't imagine flitting around him like flies.

And if she was thinner now, Charlie would see to that later, when he had her back laughing in the throes of him, with Johnny coming down in the morning to shake his head at them, behind her back, their secret, too, about a woman who was well-loved.

What more could she want? But of course it was premature to ask this now, by which knowledge he too was attached, for many reasons, to Darrell by a string, as children who tie together evaporated milk cans and hide with them behind trees.

Then, one day, by surprise, like a light flickering, Irene realized that neither Ida, nor Arlene, nor Ruby *had* sons old enough yet to be in the war. For how many afternoons had she listened to them in the background pop their mouths with their thumbs, calling, "Bam, bam" at their sisters or brothers younger still?

She gently rested the receiver into its cradle, saying, "Dumb, dumb," and tapping her forehead before indignation rose in her throat: a caught bug or a fish bone which wouldn't dislodge. Of course Ruby listened to T.V. and could talk about making pie for dinner!

But worse, where had she *been*, when everything in her depended on what her body could sense, of the air and what was bearing its way toward her? She shook her head like a dog who had wandered into a clover-patch of bees. She wanted to run outside to the barn, to tell Charlie, to *ask* him. . . .

And so she was at the front door when the red pick-up truck drove into the dirt drive, Rufus walking across the road from the milking barn, Charlie and Johnny behind him, as if *they* knew the truck was coming, had to come, came by appointment.

She almost fell over the hoe left outside in the clump of canna lilies; her body jostled so that, for a minute, she was sure she wasn't seeing what she was seeing: Rufus's wife (since who else would drive up like that) getting out of the cab of the pick-up and three boys, coffee-colored like Rufus, jumping over the tail gate behind her.

Rufus raised his good arm in greeting, which made her look at the boys lined up like steps, one almost big enough to be in Korea, two of them—she saw this in a flash of recognition as of a place she had been to—with their left arms short, a little cupped hand sticking out below each short sleeve where the elbow should have been.

Irene stopped, her mouth opened, all she had wanted to say for months beginning to assemble. And then, to hold her voice back, which might explode before them, she ran to Rufus's wife and reached to hold her, both arms around her neck, then reaching down to beat her on the back, Irene either laughing or crying—Charlie would never be sure—caught in the extremity of—what?

For when at last Charlie and Johnny managed to pull her away, on her face was etched a look of pure repose which, so foreign to them, resembled ferocity, applicable at any time.

Goodbye, Goodbye

When Sukie ran away—monarch cracking Spring's cocoon—first came Ida, clothes proffered first to tell us how she saw herself, "Lady in Small Prints," regardless her church circle had taken to modern fibers, color of pajamas, tops the shape of bowling shirts. And Ida didn't envision her body from my vantage point at the screen, her high rump hiking the field of dress in the back, veins a thatch of blue on the lily backs of her knees, and one embedded flower of black. Her shoes were brown, with straps, and on her head sat a white straw hat with peonies. Bobby's sapphire poked through the string of her pink crocheted gloves.

"He couldn't come," called Ida, as if the brilliance on her left hand was all I saw when, for a second, I imagined Bobby's transmission spread tagged all over their swept yard, bantams pecking at his can of tools.

"Well just look at you," said Momma as she climbed the rise. "Church clothes. And to what, pray tell," (Momma gearing up) "do we owe this pleasure?" Momma, underestimating, wore slacks.

So Ida stopped, casserole held out, lace of her collar flipping in the April breeze. Her sapphire-blue eyes for which Bobby bought the ring went wild for a second, and, it seemed, as she looked down at our tiny house, they asked, "Is this-here the place, of tragedy, infirmity, disaster, disgrace, or whatever they want to call it?" Then Ida sniffed the pollen-laden air. "Who's Rhea kidding?" the nose said.

But Momma was not kidding. She had, after tearing up Sukie's half of our room to unearth a clue, summoned everyone related for miles around. She held the phone near her heart, looking up at the mirrored wall before dialing as if the Apostles coagulated there like silver. She squinted her eyes, wrinkled her nose.

And so our multiple saviors came: Charlie and Tommy and Ralph, Paul, Irene, Ida, "all them," as Momma would say, taking on their coloration: twitters, trills, puffed feathers of warning.

You could forget, then, Momma had ever been to school, played the violin once, piano on the side, or had been so lovely small boys stared. Except when Momma lapsed, her body was as graceful as linen falling; hands, the resting necks of swans.

Then, with the house full, it was a party with what they made best: corn casserole (Ida); tuna and noodles with mushroom soup, fried onion on the top; vanilla pudding with strawberries; three-bean salad; raspberry jello with canned pineapple chunks. Momma opened the gate-leg table in front of the living room windows, and they put the food there. His cow-lick dipping as he stooped, Tommy hoped out loud the dog wouldn't run into one of the legs.

Charlie flattened the couch; Tommy, glancing out the back bedroom window, noticed the clothesline sagged and went to fix it. "What else you got needs fixed?" he called, but Momma didn't hear him, nor notice that, when he'd gathered up all the dog's bones, he sat beside them, smoking his Camels, knees at his chest, arms around them, one hand cupping the cigarette as he'd learned in Korea, breezes blowing or not.

In the living room, Momma circled the dog, saying, "Shoo, shoo," as if the dog were bovine, and the dog acting as if we were to be rounded up. Ida took off her hat, put it on top of the pine cupboard over the bust of Luther, and said maybe Momma ought to sit and think.

"Think? Think!" said Momma. Her voice was a lute, an oboe, a violin, taking on first one section of a score, then another as, I think, she let pictures of Sukie flit past her eyes: Oh Lost and Wandering, Ivy Trailing, Smell of Honeysuckle, Shimmer of Willow, the cascading moon.

And when last *did* we see her? Charlie asked that, little note pad in his huge hands, stub of a pencil poised.

"*Eons* ago," said Momma, waving one hand as if to encompass the dank cave, women in straw hair, men's clubs held high, and firelight flitting on the drawings.

"Call James," said Irene, strawberry juice on her navy skirt, one red nail picking at it.

"James? James!" shrieked Momma, all she felt for and against

Poppa percussion tapping her ribs, everyone going silent to hear such passion resonate.

"Well it was *just* a thought," said Irene.

Then, after respectful silence, Ralph slapped one knee. "So!" He brightened, hearing his own voice. "What can we *do* for you, Rhea?"

"Do? Do!" I said to myself in Momma's stead. But she surprised me, putting her chin on her chest, looking out the cafe curtains past all the food, and drawing the word out like a train whistle from far off. "Do-o-o-o?" which, coming closer, was a howl.

As if Sukie were in Tucson or Daytona Beach or, as Momma would have said, "One of Them Places," the whole world spat out.

In the timbre, Irene rolled her eyes at Ralph, and soon Ralph put on his navy windbreaker and got in the Dodge van to go driving the streets of Greenville while listening to the ball game, keeping one eye out for Sukie on, as he considered it, the left-field chance.

And, had he seen her then, it would have been as if she'd stood in the stands to catch a fly ball, her flounced white skirt looking like so many shirts, back then when men came in suit coats and, second inning, removed their jackets, ties dangling to their knees—Ralph's era, so what could he, I thought, have known of Sukie's ardent heart?

The rest of us ate a little of this and that, except Tommy in the yard, his Camel cold in his lips and his eye shut, ears hearing, I would have bet, each word.

Flies hovered over the napkins Momma had put on the dishes, some dipping into the spaces by the spoons. "No one brought chicken," Ida said to the dog, "and even then you wouldn't of got any."

"We forgot the blessing!" Momma cried, coming from the bathroom. "*Lord,*" she added, meaning the last straw.

Late in the afternoon, the loudest sound the clock atop Sukie's piano, Momma did her nails, one hand spread on the sofa arm, polish clinched between her knees.

"Her hands don't even shake," Ida said to Irene, by her on the other end of the sofa, Ida's head listing.

"And where the hell is Ralph?" Irene whispered, presumably not to awaken Charlie on the rug. Ida's strapped feet rested on his overalls.

"I still say call the police," Ida announced to us all.

"You"—Momma pointed with one fuchsia nail—"have got to be crazy. Sheesh, 'the police.' " She blew on her nails.

"It was *her* thought," said Irene, "but it was still just a thought."

Then Ralph came back, trailing through the long grass what appeared to be a dog. "Look what I found," he said at the door, plopping it down, shoving its hind end so that its paws made a skittering sound on the semi-circle of tile. "Out on Easley Bridge Road. I about kilt it and then I thought, 'Why not bring it to Rhea?' "

Momma stood up. "Now Ralph," she said, voice patient and without guile, "what would I want with yet another dog?" Ours sniffed its own tail; Ralph, the mongrel, and our dog filled the space between the living room and the path to the kitchen, Ida behind Ralph, trying to look over his shoulder.

No one answered Momma. Ralph had his foot by the dog's tail, he eased it over, and when the foot pressed down and the mongrel squeaked, Irene hopped up to gather it in her arms. "Ralph," she cried, "how could you *be* so mean?"

Ralph splayed his fingers before him, car keys dangling from his ring finger. "I'm not mean," he said, voice small, like a child singing in church. He backed into the kitchen, rubbing the bald spot on his head.

Paul, I thought, was missing it all, his snore a fly buzzing the drape of his lips. Then, maybe not. At five-thirty he came from the back bedroom, rubbing his face. But his eyes were clear. "Honey, forgive me, but I gotta get. I hear them cows bellowing from here."

We all cocked our ears.

"So *soon*?" Momma cried, looking up at Paul, his head almost touching the low ceiling. Then Momma clapped her hands together. "Let's not, then, stand for thinking anything's *sacred*."

And she went to the piano, pulling out Sukie's bench, and flipped the lid—this sacrilege of which Momma knew each crease.

She riffled through pages of Bach, Rachmaninoff, arrangements by Van Cliburn or, at least, sheets of music with his face at twenty on the front. "Is that all she's got?" Momma asked us all. "She thinks we can let Paul go milk his cows on *that*?"

Paul put a hand on Momma's shoulder. "Rhea?"

"Oh, it's hopeless," said Momma, burrowing her head between her arms, arms laid across the keys so softly only a concordance of notes came out. Then Momma cried. We heard her sobs waft up.

"I knew it, I knew it," said Irene, standing with the dog cradled in her arms. "*And*," she said to Ralph as if Momma's sobs gave license, "*I'm* taking this dog home."

At the door Paul said to Momma's curved back, "Didn't mean to start a stampede. Tell you what—I'll send over a quart of Jersey by one of the boys. How's that?" He peered down to look at what would be Momma's eyes if her head hadn't been turned. "Hope you find her," he added, backing out.

Which is what they all called as they drove off, caravan of departing consolation. But it lit on the trees: "Find her, find her." The sound didn't stop at the door. "*We have to find her*," said Momma, words measured as if to Sukie's metronome.

Her face looked indented, her mascara ran. But the voice was her own again, reluctant, as if measuring the air each word would take.

"We will, Momma," I said.

"I will," I said to myself. And, as the light closed down, I gathered up all they'd left: Paul's cigars on the nightstand, Ida's crocheted gloves, too pink, Irene's package of Winstons, a lighter with a poodle on it, and the serving spoons.

Momma went to stretch herself out on the sofa, her bony, stockinged feet up on one arm, her arms crossed behind her head, cupping her reddish hair. I closed the piano lid, so softly.

"Read to me," she said, eyes shut, her jazzy self tamped down by every breath. "Browning," she added, meaning the wider world of Robert, other times. And as I read, Momma slept, I think, or his words so released her tongue saliva trickled from her mouth loosened for repose.

Later, when I heard her snore, I pulled the phone into the bedroom, and, sitting on Sukie's bed, called Poppa at the news bureau, Orlando, Florida.

"Sweets," he said, "what we've got here is an international crisis. So find her." And when I asked what crisis, he said not to worry my dark little head. Years later, when I visited, he added, "So I got on the plane with the team going to Cuba, looked around, felt the damn thing shake, and I said, 'Hold it, Boys,' and went in and bought myself some more insurance. Thought, 'Hell, if I'm going out, at least let the girls live it up in style,' " which is to say he thought of us. His voice, as Momma snored, made our plight as feathers on a wing. And *he* knew Sukie was near, as if, had he not been distracted, he could have plucked her up.

Then, that week, to prove Poppa right, the local bills began to come, from Belk-Simpson, J. C. Penney, Sears Roebuck. For hats.

"Hats?" asked Momma, her voice weak. "Hats?" She shut her eyes, trying to picture Sukie covering her gold-tapestry hair, it flipping at the ends around a feather or resting beneath a brim of straw. Years later Momma would write in a letter, "We blonds have to be careful," when Momma never was a blond.

All week on the phone I heard her ask, "Hats?" and, "Are you sure it wasn't a chemise?", her voice improving with each call until, with Ida or Irene, it was a rodeo call, "Hats!" And when she put down the phone, she came in where I sat reading on the sofa, saying, "Hats! It don't make sense."

"Doesn't," I said. "It *doesn't* make sense."

Then Momma stopped—this minute edge of time I have frozen in my mind. She wondered, I think, where I 'd been all that time, as if I'd hunkered with Tommy in the yard. And then she rushed at me, her eyes dark with fury, and beautiful, as I think of them. She pushed me back against the sofa, throwing my book aside. "Don't you *ever* think for a minute I don't know the difference." She pushed again. "You understand? And they did, too, once. You understand?"

But did I, then?

With the bills piling up on the table under the windows, Paul and Tommy and Charlie, Ralph, Irene, and Ida began to drop by weekday afternoons, bringing money in little church envelopes, which they slipped on top of the piano. And, once, a hat box for Momma, filled with miniature hats such as dolls or party-goers wore. Momma's eyes widened, as if Sukie hid there. She shuddered, opening it. Tommy slapped her on the back, saying, "Joke, Rhea, joke!"

Then Momma laughed. She tied on her head the silvery blue one left over from a New Year and danced around the room. "Who does Sukie think she *is?*" Momma asked, twirling in laughter around Tommy, the handsome one. And Irene held the mongrel to give them room.

After that, we left the screen door unlatched so, at any time, they could come in—Paul with his quarts of milk or Ida with her casseroles and sewing, after Momma taught her, those long days of waiting. Or Tommy, stopping by on his way to play bingo at the VFW Hall.

I had no time to read to Momma then, and she didn't ask. "She'll come when she comes," she said, playing cards with Charlie, who stayed on after Paul went to milk his cows. "*If* we don't go broke," said Charlie, to which Momma said, as if they were toothpicks on the table, "Oh, *hats.*"

Who was Momma, now?

Of course I found Sukie. I followed her from Belk-Simpson, or followed the swinging box and the boy in uniform from Ft. Wayne on her other arm, the creases in his pants not so very sharp.

On her head was nothing but the sun of her hair.

Followed her up the flights of stairs over Renquist's Jewelry, and heard her giggle behind the door: what she had, having strayed from music.

At home, Ida sat with Momma and Bobby in the yard, a watermelon in the circle their bodies made, Momma holding one slice to her mouth and waving to me with the other hand. "Look who we got here!" Momma called, punching Bobby with one hand. His pick-up was parked on the rise, looking almost new.

I sat on the sofa with my plate of watermelon, looking out the screen, thinking.

Toward dusk they came in and sang around the piano—Ida's music: hymns. Momma's hands ran up and down the keys as revivalists' did in August, which Momma had hated: the unrestrained. Bobby had his banjo.

And, of course, I went in to visit Sukie, waiting at one end of the dark hall until the boy from Ft. Wayne left.

"Who pays?" I asked, that first.

And Sukie laughed. "Him! Arnie! Who else?"

In the room was a bed, a chest of drawers, a chair, and Sukie's boxes of hats. "Not for the hats," I said.

"Well he can't pay for everything!" said Sukie, turning her beautiful self before the mirror, feathers curved around her neck, her long fingers spreading one feather across her brow.

"Momma will kill you," I said, not knowing, now, if it were true.

Then Sukie turned, her cotton dress swirling as she turned. She came to sit by me on the bed. She took my hands in hers, which she had never done. She held them still and looked me in the eyes. She hissed, "We will *suffocate* if we go back."

"Not me," I said. "I won't suffocate."

"Oh yes you will." She smoothed down her dress, and my hands sat limp in my lap. "You will," the last word long with breath as if life pulled up in box cars.

And, at home, Ida was cooking, Paul was cutting grass, and Momma: singing.

"Do you love him?" I asked one day when Arnie had left, wondering as I asked if I would love someone like him.

"Heavens no," said Sukie, "he's just a boy." And she went to the window, to lean out, looking down at the shoppers hurrying below, where, too, maybe Paul was driving through afternoon traffic to get to Momma's for supper. Maybe Charlie rode shot-gun and planned to take her to a drive-in theater after they ate, the three of them, with popcorn, Momma in the middle.

Maybe Arnie returned that night, and maybe he didn't, Sukie contenting herself with night's high-yellow falling into silence.

Then came the week in which I knew she wasn't coming back.

I was walking along Main Street when the first hat fell, the straw with black ribbons. Watching it sail, I looked up over Renquist's canopy and saw her right arm held out as if she waved. And still I ran to get it, amidst honking horns and a driver calling, "Watch it, kid."

And on the stairs I dusted it off, smoothed down the ribbons, tried it on, finding a thread of elastic under the brim, which I wouldn't have imagined.

"*No, Silly,*" said Sukie when she opened the door and saw me holding out her hat.

She let me follow her to the window, let me watch the arc her thin arm made, and watch the people looking up. I heard her giggle.

"See?" she asked, and then, I think, forgot me while looking down, her hair spread across her shoulders. I closed the door, so softly!

All week, hidden under the canopy, I watched her fling her hats, sometimes three in a row as if inspired. I imagined Arnie watched her too, standing behind the post of Woolworth's entrance while sipping a cherry-flavored Coke. And all I imagined saying in words, to myself or to Poppa or to whoever sat around Tommy at the bingo table was, *It's still a lot of money down the drain.*

I saw Arnie after that, wandering in and out of the news stand. And, one day, I brought him home. On the way, I made him promise not to breathe a word. I *almost* held his hand.

And Momma liked him. She let him eat with us. Tommy took him with him to a ball game Ralph was coaching, in his navy suit pants to match his windbreaker. Bobbie let Arnie help him fix the truck, and Irene said he reminded her of Ralph before Ralph's hair began to thin.

Sukie wrote from Atlanta, by and by, little note cards with an illegible address, saying she was fine. Reading the first one, Momma said to Ida, "Well, then!" and played a hymn or two especially loud until Paul, who knew her best, said, "Rhea?"

Did Poppa have a web around him, arms and legs and music, any kind?

And I began to suffocate.

I call Momma now and then, in my separate place miles apart from anyone I know. We talk above the sound of the dog Arnie brought, to which Momma said, "Oh, why not, what with Irene's mutt and all," and above the sound of Ida cooking, apron pinned to her prints. Or of Charlie mowing grass and, sometimes, Bobby's banjo. Even of the flowers growing, laundry flapping in the breeze.

At night I ask, for Sukie, and for me stretched out in vanity and hope: Do we not think, if we could find one person strong enough alone to mop our beading brows, in perfect quiet, we would call that love?

Voice

It was the season when odors rose like invisible flame against the landscape of suffocating heat. Beneath the burnt grass and withered kudzu, rodents, skunks, knots of insects were dying, for we saw daily buzzards circling the folds of the hills. The hills lay belly-up and reddish against the skyline, the kudzu, with nothing to hold it, having slipped like a robe downward. As if to anchor these dead or sleeping Buddhas, an occasional tree rose from their navels. Without the trees, they might have rolled down into the valley, leaving the horizon deserted and more still.

We waited and, although we were accustomed to waiting, this time it seemed to be for something ineffable, as for a revelation heat promises when it becomes intense enough to purify.

Other times we had waited in towns, tethered, it seemed, at a carnival we might join.

I was ten then. I think, now, that nerve-endings can become fecund, sprout in a perfect coupling of time, place, our suspended bodies.

We needed ragged time, and freedom.

Claire was twelve that summer, her one chant: "You don't know the *half* of it," meaning the lives of our parents in whom, so casually lodged, our freedom gestated.

There was, then, time which came in waves—the barking of dogs owned by a neighbor so far away we had not met, as if his roaming hounds were his surrogate into our world. And at noon came the mail truck on the valley road, its sound coming in crests as it wove through the stands of trees where farmers kept stills—on clear nights we had seen wisps of smoke punctuating the moonlit silence. We got no mail, drank no moonshine.

At three in the afternoon, the royal blue bus of The Church of the Holiest Redeemer ("How many Redeemers *were* there?" our mother asked) rumbled over the hills near our house, empty of children already delivered home from Bible school in Greer.

Then, at twilight, rose the cacophony of crickets, and frogs venturing from their panoply of thatch. I couldn't eat their legs when our mother cut them loose for our supper, throwing their scaly bodies in a cardboard box by the two-eyed stove. Perhaps I thought their voices were unsullied, would rise from the box to admonish me for hunger.

My bare feet padding in the red dust of the road to the deserted house across from ours was another sound, mid-mornings when I went to sit on the porch, a look-out, the old farm-house sitting on the rise from which anything approaching was visible.

And where was Claire when the morning sun hit the tin roof of our one-room house, a flare in the opaque heat? She slept on, I thought, for her appearance that summer was of someone drugged with sleep, her gold hair matted, dark and wet at the ends as if she chewed it in a dream of fury. Or, I sometimes thought, she never slept, learning by every sound what our parents had planned. Our mother whimpering in what she imagined as her privacy? Or getting up in the middle of the night to make lists of where one might go? Did Claire see our mother remove her housedress, was her body still beautiful?

Like our dog, Claire rarely made a sound. But, unlike the dog, whose fur matted with burrs our father would hate when he saw her again, Claire did not roam. She was a shadow of our mother, popping up behind her like the India-rubber ball I had read about. What *was* her use to our mother?

He would arrive sometime during the summer—Father, who had set us here and would retrieve us in his own time: California time, of being at the right spot at the right time, as he had taught us was the way the rich world ran. I had no idea but from movies what he meant: the black DeSoto of the heroine rounding the mountain curve unaware that ahead of her the truck with no brakes careened toward her; the phone which rang one second after the man in the double-breasted suit pulled the trigger.

I watched the road. I would call it waiting for the dénouement but I know, now, it is yet to come.

Our house had been built by our paternal grandfather as the place where our grandmother and the eight children would wait while he built the rock house in the valley. In the little house there was no flooring, and so at night we laid our pallets on clay, which seemed by contrast cool as spring water. Sometimes I lifted the quilt to lay one leg against the clay itself. But Claire was right—what did I know, especially of luxury.

We lived, said Claire, on Father's residuals, and it would be years before I knew they were a form of tender.

Father, the last of the children, had been born in the rock house, its christening. And it, in turn, had bestowed on him his looks, which our mother said led him straight to Hollywood. Meaning what, when all of us were beautiful? This I asked Claire, who rolled her eyes in her head, shaking it in despair of ignorance such as mine.

Was our mother proud of him?

We were not to start the stove with pages from his copies of *Variety* stacked by the boxes of books in a corner. "Don't touch them," he'd said, raising one finger, looking each of us in the eyes. "Don't touch them," our mother had echoed as his maroon Nash Ambassador pulled from the roadside.

His teeth were perfectly straight and white. In sleep he ground them together all night in a rhythm, and we never forgot the sound.

The birds, too, made a covenant of sound. If, flaring up from the trees, they swooped down to sheet the yard in black and tawny wings, rain would come.

In that miasma, I stand Claire on the hard ground by our mother's garden where, in fact she must often have stood as our mother, on her knees, rooted out weeds and insects from the tomato plants, lifting even the furry leaves of squash to search underneath. I must have watched Claire from the farmhouse porch, one finger in my book (for we believed in books) and, in the absence of color, rested my eyes over and over on her white dress, that wisp at the garden's edge. She looked over the hillside in pure motionlessness.

"I knew a woman lovely in her bones," I would read much later in a book by Roethke; and I know the poem goes on. It should end there.

Then neighbors came. We had gathered in the night at our front window to watch the man unload a pick-up as our dog, refusing still to bark, raced back and forth on the dirt road. It was, I think, the only time he ever used the front door, propping it open with a stump from the yard. Someone ("It's a woman," our mother said) turned on all the lights, and, although it was only nine o'clock, we didn't light our Coleman lanterns in answer. We lay back down, listening to the sounds coming in from the window above our pallets. Before I slept again I heard our mother say, "Well," by which I knew anything could happen, a word so airborne.

They were not like us, which I knew first upon discovering his stains of tobacco juice on the road and then, later, when the woman did my hair. She had come over to ask our mother if she might put their name on our mailbox. "Certainly," our mother said, and, walking back up the path to the farmhouse, the woman repeated, "Certainly, certainly." At the steps of the farmhouse, where I had not gone since the couple moved in, she turned on me: "Look at you." She lifted my braids in both hands, on which the nails were the brightest pink, and sighed, dropping them. "*Lord*. Well come on in." And so I followed her, or followed the smell of Juicy Fruit gum and perfume and the click of her high-heeled sandals on the faded linoleum. Her yellow hair swayed across her back.

Toward twilight, coming out of the house just as the last sun hit the rise above our house, I almost stumbled, my eyes readjusting to the light, my head still hot from her hair drier. In my ears was her voice and in my mind's eye were the names of lotions and sprays on the vanity with its red crepe-paper skirt.

I walked down the steps as if a crown rested on my head. The husband drove past as I stood on the roadside. His face looked dark and sullen in the shade of the truck's roof, and I heard him slam the truck door as I opened the door to our house.

Inside, Claire, sitting on our mother's quilts with her back against the wall, touched our mother with one toe and said, "Look," lifting her chin up at me.

"A bee hive," our mother said. "A bee hive." And, putting down her book and getting up to drag me outside to the rain barrel, she said, "Wouldn't you know, wouldn't you know." And, with water, she sealed into my head all I had heard and seen—the most ordinary things, I know now: the lure our mother feared.

It rained once, the cracks in the ground filling and overflowing into a thousand rivulets, ditches, and gullies full of sound the reddish water made as it raced down to the valley where the rock house sat crumbling. For a week Claire and I did not have to bring water from the spring, but I went to look at it overflowing to the creek nearby, our gourd dipper stuck on a tree limb out of reach. When the rain stopped, worms lay atop the ground, dazed or dead, and the birds loosened themselves from the trees to feast. Watching the birds, I realized that I had not noticed them just before the rain, either distracted by the novelty of neighbors or it wasn't true—birds as heraldic.

She, Mrs. R. C. Campbell, had nailed a sign on the tree by the porch: Salon of Beauty, and another almost like it by the cut-off to the road the postman used.

"Ha!" our mother said, seeing the sign. But perhaps Mrs. Campbell thought the postman would tell people on his route and, now that it had rained, they would—the women and girls like me—feel like fixing themselves up.

Our mother had, the first evening of the three-day rain, opening for the first time the trunks which sat along the walls. I had been playing in the creek until dark. As I came into the house, my dress and hair dripped around my feet. Our dog stood shaking behind me at the open door. And there she was, pulling on hose. When she stood to ask

Claire if the seams were straight, our dog barked once as if a stranger were in the house. She held the emerald Father had given her, letting it sway on the chain, her dress its color, and she sat on the pallet by Claire so that Claire could hook it.

"How do I look, you two?" our mother asked.

I closed the door, and for minutes there was only the sound of the drops falling from the sashes of my dress, and of our mother waiting.

"You look fine, Momma," said Claire. And, hearing Claire's voice then, I thought that Claire was somehow older than our mother; she waited for nothing.

I can no longer remember whether or not our mother took off her dress then, or if it was Claire who unclasped the necklace, or when, that night, our mother slept.

Sometimes we waken with passion for someone we've loved, say under our breaths, "Please come flying," meaning *now, now, now*, to catch a truth which would transform. But the time passes, having nothing to do with how another person moves.

Then, when the sky was washed and kudzu robed the hills again, Father drove up, all of California and states between on his windshield—gray feathery splats—and across the front, a grille of feathers. He wore his pin stripe suit, the gray hat, and a grin. "Hello, Sweets," he said as I climbed from the tree, "been holding down the fort?" He brought with him steaks from the A & P on the outskirts of Greer and, spread out on the back seat, all he had taken to pawn for gas on the trip out—the cufflinks with ruby eyes, our mother's violin, the Chinese vase, and the autoharp.

That night he said, "*Make* her eat," to our mother, but I knew: if Claire ate what we ate, protruding from the inside we would see the perfect shape of steak.

From our place that night on the Nash Ambassador's fold-down bed, Claire said, "When he makes love to her and nothing happens, he takes her over against a wall and bangs her against it until something does. I bet you didn't know that."

And did she wait to see the walls of our house shake?

Of course he met the neighbors—Raymond, who worked at the West End Mill in Greer when he wasn't helping tend his father's cows on the other side of Greer. And Joyce, who said she didn't know a thing about it when our father, having gone to inspect the rock house, noticed a chifferobe missing from the room he had been born in.

"They're just poor white trash," he said, "but they've got a phone."

Did Joyce say to Raymond when he came in from work that night, "He wears this double-breasted suit and blue shirt with a white collar and cuffs and cuff links in the shape of snakes with little red eyes, you know? And a tie, all the time, in this weather. He don't even sweat."

I think not.

And I would like to have told her, It's all the clothes he's got. But our mother would not let me cross into their yard.

If I imagine the land we occupied then, from high up, as a buzzard or a hawk sees, I envision her back yard where the clothes line swayed empty in the morning breeze. The well would be there, its cover weathered and gray, and two oak trees overshadowing the house. Her shop must have been in the back room where she had taken me; its door opened onto the back porch.

I think first, she walked to the front windows to look out at our car parked on the rise, and, seeing our heads, she may have waited for the car doors to slam, morning heat filling the space in which Claire and I had slept. Then, barefoot, she would have walked over the cool linoleum to her shop and, opening the bottle of Evening in Paris, spread it on the backs of her legs. She would take the net off her hair, slip on her shorts and the pink halter, strap on the sandals, and look at herself in the vanity mirror.

The door would not slam behind her, and, I think, she would tiptoe across the porch. She might trail one hand along the clothes-line, spit on the black mark the wire made on her palm. She would walk past the tree to the left, and, over time, make a path through the weeds to the road. If it were especially hot, gnats might round her eyes, and so she would lift one hand and fan, her nails catching the light.

By then, we would be positioned: I in the tree, our father washing the car or raising the flag on the mailbox, our mother in the garden, stooping or pulling behind her the section of cardboard on which she knelt, Claire standing apart but near her. Across the valley, the bus would be heading toward Greer, empty but for the driver, whistling hymns.

Down the road she would come, swinging her arms, her hips swaying, her shoes making little eddies of dust, and her nails the only moving color below her waist. Her halter held her breasts tight, but above them the flesh quivered, like that of a new bird, still featherless.

Sometimes she stopped to talk to our father; other times, she lifted her chin and looked at a point beyond his head, as if searching the sky for a kite or a blimp.

"Out for a little airing?" our father might say.

"You're going to burn up in that suit-coat," she might answer.

Below the rise, our mother would turn her head once, sniffing the humid air, and Claire's pinafore would ruffle as she turned toward the hills.

Sometimes Mrs. Campbell wore all white, and the shorts looked homemade. I think across the hall from the room she called her shop there was a sewing machine left by whoever owned the house. Raymond might sleep to the sound of the treadle.

Of course our father used the Campbell's telephone. He sat after breakfast at the card table and made notes on cards he carried in his breast pocket. Copies of *Variety* sat where the dishes had been. On the cards he wrote: *Jay Smith: Pilot!* and *WLAC: Paul Allen, mgr.* Then, late in the morning, when the sun was as hot as it would be, he crossed the road.

"Thanks, kindly," we could hear him call, later, as he came down the steps. But what she answered, we couldn't hear. Maybe, at first, she said softly, "Any time," and he winked at her, turning. Then she might have whispered it to herself, her right hand rubbing the frayed wood of the screen.

We waited daily to hear the rattle of Mr. Campbell's truck. I had seen men come from the cotton mill; tiny balls of cotton clung to their clothes, and I imagined Raymond leaning over her hand, where a splinter might have stuck, light suffused through the wisps of cotton as she said, "Shoot, shoot, shoot, it *hurts*."

By the creek where Claire and I had taken the dog to clean her fur of burrs and wash her because our father had said we had to, though it was useless, Claire stopped to drink spring water from the dipper. Over its rim she looked at me for a long time, I think, before I sensed her eyes on my back. She must have been deciding to tell me.

"If," she said, "he does it to her, I'll kill her."

"Kill who?" I asked.

"Mrs. R. C. Campbell! Who else?"

And so I waited; my body waited, seemingly still but learning of its own accord its fragile parts. When our mother asked where we two might next be in school, and our father said, "Not in Greer, by a long shot, with boys such as Raymond once was," I knew it was where I *should* be—with them whose boots laced tight and on whose hands pads of calluses grew. This Claire taught me.

Then Joyce did something she should not have done. She must have carried the picture of our mother in her eyes or looked over at her each day she rounded the bend by the garden. Studying. Or, when it was too hot to move, she lay on a chenille bedspread or on the linoleum itself and leafed through magazines, looking up now and then to envision that which she could never be.

For, one afternoon, when she had not, that morning, taken her walk or received our father with his handful of cards, she walked to our garden, looking like someone else.

Our father sat in a folding canvas chair under the chinaberry tree, our mother was pulling the last of the tomatoes, Claire walking beside her with the lard bucket. I had followed Mrs. Campbell from my tree and stood to one side, looking.

She had dyed her hair brown, like our mother's, and cut it, curled it into a page-boy such as our mother wore. Her nails were clean of polish, and she wore a printed dress; a slip showed from underneath when she clasped her hands before her as she breathed deeply, stilling herself.

"I wonder," she said, her voice soft, "if y'all'd care to come over for tea? Under the trees, maybe. I could spread a cloth."

Then our mother was smiling wryly, all that her face had gathered into it over the weeks breaking open. She almost giggled, one hand at her mouth.

"I think not," she said. "But thank you for the invitation."

Our father did not, then, wink at Mrs. Campbell. He was watching our mother, looking at her as he might have studied a film clip enlarged in a darkened studio.

And there was nothing Mrs. Campbell could do, then, but unfold her hands and back away. Claire watched her retreating form all the way, and we heard the door close softly.

I used to think that words and music (and money, Father said) were honey outpouring; *luxury*, Claire, I would have said, borne up from any field of silence, any time. The surprises of America, which land our father loved.

But no, not even, you see, if I can imagine Mrs. Campbell's voice rising as she shows our father his part of the telephone bill, the long part, saying, "Los Angeles? New York City? Miami, Florida? and all them places?"

For three days we didn't hear his truck. We heard the dog chasing rabbits through the undergrowth, the hollow of silence left by the bus when Bible school was over, and the sound of the mail truck, which came up our road now when the flag was up. At night: crickets, our mother humming, Claire eating dry cereal from the box.

Then, on the third day, when we were packing boxes for the move to Lexington, Kentucky, WYAX, said the letterhead, our mother lifted her head from a trunk, saying, "She must have left."

We did not answer her.

It was dark outside now. The dog circled the house, then came panting to sit outside the door. We heard her turning around three times, then settling. Our mother tried on clothes from the trunk, turning to ask, "How's this, Jim?"

It was almost our bedtime. We would sleep in the absence of light from the farmhouse, and the Nash Ambassador would seem colder. Claire would lock the car doors.

Then Raymond, kicking out at the dog, I think, came bursting in. His face was tight, as if his teeth held the skin on, and his body looked larger than it was from where we sat on the quilts. He stopped at the doorway, looking down once at our father, and then to our mother, who half-rose, her rose-colored dress shining in the light of the lanterns. I don't think that he spoke. It was the kind of quiet one hears in a church before the baptismal immersion, when, in sympathy, everyone holds his breath. He looked for a minute at our mother, as if the color of her dress filled his eyes.

Then he saw Claire, standing now with her back against the wall by the trunk, which made a shadow on her legs. She wore a cotton slip; light shone on it and on her skin, so white that it seemed the slip was part of her skin.

He looked at her for a long time, and it was as if only they were in the room. Then he shivered, his body, it seemed, saying: You didn't expect it.

His chest seemed to sink, air escaping from every pore. He grew smaller and his eyes changed—they darkened and, for a second, shut tightly. While his eyes were shut, he reached for the door knob and, without lifting his head again, he closed the door behind him. We heard him run.

I wish now, thinking of Claire, we had let her go with him. I imagine a day in the heat of August. His mouth would be dry, always now, and somehow cool. She would be standing quietly, as she does, by a chinaberry tree, where a slight wind might lift her blond hair. "First things first," he would say, his only words, and pulling her against his chest, they would hear the beating of wings in the seal of one another's ribs. And the cry we would have to imagine would set us free.

Andantino

Roselle was tired of the piano, tired of planks of notes which began each score. She was left, then, to build whole edifices. When she was through for the day, she'd look at her hands expecting them to be raw. She felt orphaned, too, tossed into the cold, though it was never cold where they lived.

Sitting in the winged-back chair with his newspaper and hearing Roselle sigh, Frank said, "Well, Honey, why not just quit, now that I've got the third dealership open?" This, since the small amount of money Roselle made was not the question, was Frank's way of saying he loved her either way, with music or without.

He'd found her in Escanaba, Michigan during her rest cure, after her mother's death. He'd said upon looking into her eyes and at the pouches of gray beneath them, "Well! It's obvious you've got to give up the big stuff"—meaning Tanglewood, Wolftrap, her long and flowing dresses, about which Roselle had talked so tentatively. "Play where the *kids* can hear you, like here"—Eddie's Lounge, where Roselle had been sipping coffee when Frank came upon her. Hamburgers 50¢, a consideration to Roselle when she'd spent no money without her mother's presence, and a blanket of smoke when she'd needed it, grief a spotlight.

"Me," Frank had announced in the second week of his two-week vacation. "You probably need me." And that had been true for Roselle.

Was she sad, then *and* now?

And now, if she needed a rest, from *what* would she take it?

During this summer of 1959, Roselle at age 35 was prettier than she'd ever been or would be again, although no one was keeping track. Frank saw her from his chair as if she perched in a tableau of angles made by the baby grand's lifted lid, or as an outline against the dark in which they sometimes made love.

In Fort Lauderdale's off-season months, you could cut the lights in the showroom *and* the lots, leave the cars gleaming in light cast off from elsewhere, drive the quiet streets with your own lights off, and slip into bed as if the whole process were one of Roselle's rest notes.

What Frank didn't register of Roselle's habits, Roselle's mother, now that she was dead, kept with her there—wherever. For instance, how Roselle in sleep cupped her hands under her chin. *She* had watched Roselle, had given her Rachmaninoff for safe-keeping, "so misunderstood," Roselle's mother had said, pained to the quick.

The time after dinner, when Frank returned to work, Roselle thought of as her own, distinct from the daylight hours when, though he never had, Frank might come rushing in looking for papers in the secretary or in the cardboard file boxes in the laundry room. In her mind, the papers related to the black limousine for funerals or a governor's entourage or for the local campus should Borges or Auden come to read, the traveling companion behind the driver, view obstructed by the black cap.

Anything, Roselle thought, could happen in daylight, in glare, wind, the taste of salt in the air. Trees so low they were a ceiling holding up the limitless sky. Under it as if capped, she was participating in love, like anybody, was she not?

And when the season began and college kids tore into town, it grew so hot the piano keys sometimes stuck, even Roselle's fingers sticking to the keys. Then a bird of panic would flutter in her throat.

In a month they would come again—the kids—and her second year with Frank would have passed. Frank would take an extra shirt to work, he showed so many cars then. And rent for the duration a vacant lot on a side street, filling it with cars brought down from Orlando, junkers, he called them, should the kids get stranded, wire home for money, and, what the heck, blow it on a car. It was his season.

On Saturday nights at the lounge where Roselle played, Arthur, the owner, would tell Roselle to liven it up a bit, Roselle having wondered during the past season if *this* were the time for Rachmaninoff, whose music she'd never liked. Then thinking not.

Once Frank had called her on the bar phone, Roselle walking through the crowd with her heart pounding as if she had a child who might have turned sick in her absence. She pictured for a second the child's hair matted in fever. "Holding up?" Frank had shouted into the receiver.

Once, on what Roselle had thought of as an ordinary day, Frank had brought home a box from the Quality Bakery, set it on the table, flipped open the lid, lit candles, and called her to get up from the piano. "What *is* it?" Roselle had asked, afraid to move closer.

"Well *look*, Honey."

And when Roselle had looked, one hand at her throat, had seen the numerals and the one word, 1.5 YEARS, overlooking the speck of pink frosting which separated the 1 from the 5, she had believed for an instant that Frank *had* known her all that time, had been in the background just off-stage, had seen her climb onto the bench beside her mother, who worked the pedals years before anyone like Frank could have been interested.

Frank had touched a knife to the pink dot, lifted it up, saying, "That'll be us someday, Honey, and we'll have grown old together." Roselle felt her breath lower in her body, a fish's bubble in reserve.

From her sick bed, Roselle's mother had advised, "If you ever get stuck in your career, do volunteer work," which Roselle knew meant offering a master class at the local college. But having taken to wearing her mother's housedresses against the heat, Roselle could not imagine having boys in bermuda shorts and tennis shoes look at her. Or girls with mustard seeds at their necks. No matter what they imagined they wanted to know of music, Roselle was sure she could not talk loudly enough between passages for them to hear.

Instead, in the kind of restlessness which makes the brain flare, Roselle began sitting in a lawn chair on what Frank called their patio, in front of the clapboard garage from which he'd dug up the concrete and laid rows of sod, putting a white picket fence as separation from the sidewalk.

She would wear a wide-brimmed hat, one of Frank's long-sleeved work shirts, and, across her legs because she thought she ought not tan, a blue cotton sheet. She would shut her eyes and, with her left hand, reach down beside her to turn on the portable radio Frank used when one of the boys at work took him fishing.

In the garage were her boxes of sheet music and records, even of herself playing four-handed compositions with her mother, when Roselle was fifteen and her mother was trying to give her a leg-up, as she said, on the concert stage.

When Roselle dozed and would waken suddenly because a car or children on bikes rode by, in her mind would be a picture of Frank's house, containing nothing, Roselle imagined, but Frank's chair, the piano with its lid down, and the table in the alcove where they ate. No chairs, no hanging chandelier.

If she were sleeping when Frank drove up for supper, he called over the fence from where he parked his car on the street, "Hey, Rosie, I brought you something," and tossed her his *Wall Street Journal*. Then he would wink. Under the blue cotton sheet, her legs would be stuck together.

Or if he found her sleeping, Frank would call, "What's for supper?", to which Roselle would have to say, "I don't know, tuna?" But Frank would drive to the Chinese restaurant and bring little boxes of food, whistling as he spooned her portions out, as if nothing Roselle could do or neglect to do would disturb him ever.

Roselle would have put the radio on the alcove table, her sheet, hat, and his old shirt piled on the floor by her chair. Frank would look at the radio, then at Roselle, and wink the same wink, but, now, meaning what?

Those times Roselle felt as if she hadn't wakened, simply the house had grown full and she watched from her chair this happenstance.

If she asked him had he sold a car, Frank laughed, saying, "How do you think it happens? You don't sell a car every day!"

And, truly, Roselle didn't understand how it happened, Frank

68

saying she needn't worry about it a bit.

I wasn't worrying, Roselle protested to herself.

Outside, she didn't actually listen to the radio—it was a hum, mostly of voices, the timpani section, as if it practiced without the violins and oboes, louder when the commercials came on, Frank's among them recorded by Frank, but she hadn't heard it, his revving up for the season. Mostly she slept, as if waiting, or as if sleep were the only natural state.

"That's him," she thought she heard a child say one day. But when Roselle looked up, struggling to awaken as if surfacing through water, all she saw was a pair of girls on bicycles at the end of the road where the trees seemed to meet. A dream, she thought, of when I met Serkin and Momma's hands shook.

If Roselle were waiting to be gotten, there were no relatives in America to come for her, the Hungarian ones not even making it over when her mother died. "An upheaval's coming," they had written, "and we're sorry." Then it had come.

"You don't know it, but that's him," the girl *was* saying, Roselle lifting the brim of her hat to see her standing by the fence, a bag from the A & P in front of her on the sidewalk and, in the distance, the other girl turning to yell, "You're going to *get* it."

"Who are *you*," Roselle asked, keeping one hand at the brim of her hat.

"Annie."

She wore white knee socks, ribbons dangling from her braids. "And 'him'?"

The girl twirled one braid with her fingers, the other hand resting on the fence. She pointed to Roselle's radio without lifting her hand from the fence. "My daddy. That's him." She tossed her head. "And *she* thinks this is half-way, but this ain't no half-way." Then she lifted up the bag and, turning, said, "I gotta go or they'll kill me. He wouldn't like that. So bye."

The girl's white socks slipped down as she walked. Roselle watched her lean to pull one up, then walk on, the sun in her hair, Roselle noticed, making it look almost white.

On the radio, a man was reading softly, to which Roselle slept. Just before she slipped into sleep, Roselle imagined that the girl stopped to turn every few feet to see if she was listening.

Then, having tried to find the same voice on the radio when she woke, Roselle began to wait for the girl, who did not come the next day, of which Roselle was sure because she hadn't even dozed. But Roselle had come close to sleeping when, on a Wednesday, the girl, alone this time, stopped at Roselle's fence. "Turn it up, would you?"

"But he's not on," said Roselle. "I've been listening and I don't think he's on." Roselle had taken off her hat; the sun burned on her scalp where Roselle put one hand, as if to rub it in. The girl wore a dress with sashes dangling loose to the sidewalk.

"Thirteen-point-nine-on-your-radio-dial," said the girl. "I bet you don't have it on thirteen-point-nine. He don't work all over the *dial*!"

So Roselle turned the knob, past gospel music and what sounded like Frank shouting from inside a tunnel and past news of more heat. When she found the station, she turned to the girl, saying over the noise of drums, "See?"

"Well he can't be on *all* the time! He's *coming* on," and the girl looked up at the sun. "He'll *be* on. He'll be on for thirty minutes, and that's it. Mondays, Wednesdays, Fridays. And I always got to be *out* of the house if I wanta hear him 'cause Momma and her"—she nodded toward the road as if the other girl were there on her bike—"won't *let* me."

"Your sister," said Roselle, a statement, as if she knew about sisters.

"Yeah, them."

"Oh," said Roselle. Then the girl sat cross-legged on the grass between Frank's fence and the sidewalk. Roselle looked at her

70

through the slats. "Would you like to come in?"

"Ain't no way," said the girl.

"*Isn't.*"

"Isn't. And if I climbed over and tore my dress, Momma'd like to kill me."

Roselle almost added, "And he wouldn't like that," but would the girl smile? Each sentence, Roselle noticed, was a burst of sound, as if the girl's mouth clamped shut to build more steam between each sentence. And Roselle realized for the first time that Frank hadn't put in a gate.

The girl sat with her head resting against the slats of the fence — Roselle could imagine indentations sinking her forehead in. "Well," she said, "you could. . . ."

"Hush up, here he comes," said the girl, and so Roselle clamped her own mouth shut and reached down to turn up the volume. The girl smiled, then shut her eyes.

When it was over: "This is Jim with 'The time for *Us*' " — and the sun was slipping behind the trees, the girl opened her eyes and looked around, as if surprised to see Roselle. "He does that every other day," she said.

Roselle smiled as if to herself. "He reads *Sonnets from the Portuguese* and plays a little Peter Duchin between them every other *day*?"

"I don't know about Peter-whoever, but, see," the girl explained, getting up and tying her sash as she talked, "he gets to do the whole book through three times. Then that's it. Then he goes on to some other station, *if* they pay a talent fee, and he starts over. But I gotta go."

So the girl named Annie went down the street in little hops, leaving Roselle to lean her head back in the chair, taking deep breaths as if she needed them.

Sometimes Annie came at 5:00 and sometimes she didn't. She never came on the off-days and so, in deference, as Roselle thought of it, she turned the radio off. On the days when she listened to "A Time for Us" alone, it was as if Annie's eyes were on her the whole time. Or Jim's, wondering where Annie was? "You're getting tan," said Frank. "Don't burn yourself up," to which Roselle said, "I won't, I won't,"

71

the heat tingling her scalp—what the leaping fish must feel.

How many pages did Annie think were *in* the book?, Jim's voice, Roselle thought, an anodyne to music so sweet Roselle's mouth turned as if she'd eaten a persimmon or a quince.

"Why doesn't he have an accent like you do?" asked Roselle.

"Trained himself out of it," said Annie.

"Where will you go next?" asked Roselle.

"*He* knows," said Annie.

She wouldn't come inside the fence, no matter that Roselle told her how she could walk through the piano room, into the alcove, and out the side door.

"Can't," she said. "You're a stranger. You talk more like him."

"Oh," said Roselle. "So I do."

"Where're you from?"

"Lots of places," said Roselle, suddenly able to picture them all, only her mother's place inaccessible, or Budapest after the storm of fire.

So it was, when Annie listened, always she leaned her forehead against the fence slats, shut her eyes, and did not move until it was over. Sometimes at night, lying beside Frank and waiting for sleep, Roselle knew how Annie's body felt, tilted and so still the ears were all the body knew of itself.

"He has a nice voice," said Roselle.

"Everybody knows that!" said Annie. "Even them," motioning with her head to the lots beyond the trees where Roselle imagined his fat wife sat fanning herself on the porch while the sister read comics on the sofa.

On the third Saturday after Roselle had begun to listen to "A Time for Us" and Frank was letting her out of the car in front of Arthur's, Roselle said, "Don't forget—you can't call. I've got to be calm when I play even when it's nothing at all."

"Be calm," said Frank. "Be calm," smiling as he backed up, and waving.

Roselle called before he pulled away, "Sell lots of cars tonight," as if in recompense. And, all that night, she couldn't concentrate.

"I'll probably have to quit before Arthur's fills up with kids," she said when Frank came for her at 1:00.

"Well that'll be just fine," said Frank, slapping one palm on the steering wheel, settling it, and at the red lights reaching out to put a hand on her left knee.

"I'll never need to wear glasses," said Roselle, out of nowhere.

One day, listening alone, Roselle heard Jim say: "I can wade grief / Whole pools of it / I'm used to that," and, languid in the heat, near sleep, Roselle said, "You are *not*," under her breath, as if he were in a room with her. And, only so slowly, did it come to her, not what was different, but a rhythm, she said to herself—the rhythm's changed. Then, for the first time since she had married Frank, Roselle went into the garage where Frank had stored all her music and books from Roselle's mother's house, and, humming, searched until she found the book he read from now.

When Annie came next, Roselle, as she thought of it, let Annie rest her head against the slats as always, let her close her eyes. "Mine," said Jim, signing off, "while the ages steal!"

Roselle let Annie sigh, shake herself back into time.

"That," said Roselle, "is Emily Dickinson. He *finished* on the day before yesterday, *Sonnets from the Portuguese* the third time through."

"*They* don't know it," whispered Annie through the slats. "And you won't tell, will you?"—Annie looking up at Roselle as if all her breath were gone.

"Me?" asked Roselle, thumping her hot chest with her fingers. "*Me?*" And then Roselle began to laugh while Annie watched her, until Annie laughed too, Roselle's sunburnt head feeling dizzy, as if she, Annie, and Jim danced around a room.

"You know what they want?" Annie asked one Monday before Jim came on. "They want him to do *weather*. And he won't do weather if they pay him the moon."

"I expect not," said Roselle, as if she knew. But she *did* know, in his voice and in his Fort Lauderdale time running out.

"*And,*" said Annie, "they think, when the kids come down for them weeks, he can play Fats Domino. He ain't *ever* going to play Fats Domino or any of *them*. And he won't sell beer on radio time."

Roselle lifted her head to look into Annie's eyes. "Who said?"

"*Him,*" Annie shouted, flinging her head up. "Who'd you think? If he wasn't about to come on, I'd *leave*." She put her forehead back against the fence. "He don't *drink* beer, he don't *sell* beer."

"Well, don't go," said Roselle, softly.

And, as it turned out, his wife wasn't fat. Annie had walked by on a Sunday, in a church dress. When Frank saw Annie leaning over the fence, he called to Roselle, "Got yourself a little friend, I see."

"Who's he?"

"Frank," said Roselle.

"Oh," said Annie. "Anyway, I got something to show you."

So Roselle waved to Frank, went walking with Annie, down through the heat, the glare, the sound of motorcycles on Main Street. "What?" Roselle asked.

"You'll see," said Annie, leading so that *Roselle* felt like the child. "There," said Annie, pointing to an 8 by 10 glossy picture in the window of Haftery's Clothing Store for Men. "That's him."

"Oh!" said Roselle.

"Well, you shoulda known."

"Known what?" asked Roselle, one hand at the collar of Frank's shirt.

"That he's handsome!"

"I did," said Roselle to Annie. I did, Roselle said to herself.

"People write to him all the time," said Annie.

Ladies, Roselle said to herself.

"This contest—see? You vote at the drug store," said Annie,

74

pointing, "and whoever gets the most votes for March of Dimes, then that person gets a suit. He'll get it. But *even* when he gets it, even *if* it is silk, he's not staying."

At the drug store, they voted, Annie's five dimes and Roselle's three dollar bills changed into dimes.

Over ice cream, Roselle asked, "Is she fat?"

"Her, you mean?"—Roselle nodding. "No, Momma ain't fat. She's thin. She used to be pretty. And she ain't going with him when he goes. When she opens her mouth, her jaw cracks. But that ain't why she won't go."

Roselle wanted to reach over their water glasses, touch Annie's braids, and ask, "Would *you* cry?"

Or ask, "*Her*? I might run into his wife at any time from now on out?"

Then, on the last day of the quiet season, when Jim had signed off for the last time, Roselle, trained in music, suddenly rose from her chair as Annie almost disappeared down the shaded street.

Through the yard, into the house, through the alcove, the piano room, and out the front door, running and leaping, running and leaping, Roselle caught Annie by the shoulders. She said to the back of Annie's head, "You go with *him*, no matter *what*," as if passion, indefatigable, *had* a right to exist apart from judgement, ranging the world in all seasons.

Family

Who shall know
what all our mortalities are?
Dabney Stuart

It began with dogs, an increment.

And the time was autumn of 1950, when the South had begun turning tractable, aubade of progress in how asbestos houses of rainbow pastels dotted the folds of the hills—the father had watched, had walked, even, over the cement slabs just to see how they were slapping things together these days. He had also assured himself that Pauline had kept her teaching certificate current, on the outside chance, he said, she would be needing it. And he had polished the car until it shone.

Then, in time, in the one solid house, of many chimneys and gray clapboard, James Senior had set them down, this unincorporated village named Rutherfordton a tinny note. Beyond it lay the whole symphonic world. So James Senior went there.

He was, that year, 37 and handsome. Husband of Pauline, father of Rosette and of Rosette's sister Claire, and, moreover, of the boy who had died untwining himself from Rosette at the last minute though he would have preferred taking her with him to the breathless state. James Junior's emblem was impressed on Rosette's temples, two flat, pink stars.

Since Claire was lodged apart from Rosette and Pauline, with a cousin down-state where the schools were, as Pauline said, "passable," it seemed to Rosette that Claire and James Junior (Rosette's name for him when he was, in fact, nameless) looked out for one another. A timpani section with nothing else much to do.

The birds, startled that autumn by the trucks' scarves of smoke wafting North, would not take their rests on the fence or clotheslines or the flatbed truck stuck wheelless in the field. Later, when it seemed they should batten down in the frosted trees, Rosette would watch them form imperfect v's and point themselves toward, even, she would imagine, New York.

And the mongrel dogs lumbered up from porches and off steps pointing outward over the stubble. They learned, again, to tighten the muscles of their hinter-parts, legs unfurling as if over lake water. The trucks, wheels spouting creek pebbles and knots of clay, sounded the *au revoir* of their horns at the curve, hightailing it up the new by-pass. Then the tires would sing, the dogs howl.

What they delivered up there, they delivered in daylight. Nights, in Atlanta and Asheville and Charlotte, engineers unrolled their maps of impossible mountains and did not sleep. Sometimes truckers daydreamed and careened and awoke surrounded by dogs, in the ravines an impromptu jazziness.

Their own dog attached herself now to Pauline, James Senior's red hunting boots tucked unnaturally polished and soft in a baby's blanket, in a box, in a room they didn't use.

The dog was to sleep on the rose-patterned rug, by Pauline's bed, between it and Rosette's cot. To be first at the door, to authorize even the sunlit air: he'd said, James Senior, stooping to talk to the dog. A pure-bred Irish setter, papers registered in Norfolk.

And James Senior, too, had sounded his horn at the upward curve, the repainted beige Nash Ambassador almost invisible against twilight. You could hear, then, the rubato of the spotted mongrels following him as far as the state line. Rosette imagined that he stopped at a little redwood picnic table, unleashed his own map of the mountains, and lit a Camel.

From their dog heaving between them, her nose pressed to the mesh of the screen and theirs likewise above her, there issued a new sound, her body forming, it may have felt, a voice to amend James Senior's parting.

Where was he going, to have prepared them so? He had placed both hands on the backs of their heads, even the dog's, pulling them forward, even the dog, for last kisses.

Their first morning alone, before Pauline had closed off the front rooms of the house, they had left the dog whining at the parlour window as they crossed the road to establish themselves at the Post Office. Looking back, they saw her climb for the full view onto the sheet-covered Queen Anne's chair. "Will you look at that," said Pauline, shaking her head and laughing.

But to Rosette the dog appeared useless, the house of so many rooms rising around her. "We should-a let her come."

Rosette watched Pauline consider—beautiful Pauline, the dark eyes. "No," she said, "I don't think he meant that"—all James Senior had said to the dog in the language they had contrived together. "You see?" for the door to the Post Office hung open onto a little porch and, inside, on the wood floor, the mongrel dogs slept or cooled themselves, waiting for the next trucks, the tandem razzmatazz.

Even later, after they had begun school, Rosette in the back row of Pauline's classroom (the dog asleep between Pauline's desk and the children) and Pauline had issued to each child, even to Rosette, the 3 by 5 cards by which they learned together the new state law on inoculation against four diseases which otherwise would devastate—even then they did not shoo the dogs from the Post Office.

There the nurse came, in white touched off by a tiny gold pin on her flat chest, alcohol amingle with the odor of grain next door. And it was left to Rosette to place a naked arm under the iron bars of the window, expose the blue and pulsing vein as the dogs romped through the line of children. That day they sold stamps at the Feed Store counter.

James Senior wrote similar things to them both, on post cards picturing St. James Cathedral, behind which left spire would be printed such sentences as, "I take it everything is fine. Making connections apace. Kisses for you all," though he would add instructions on Pauline's cards, by which little by little Rosette was learning all that could ruin a dog.

Outside the Feed Store, the dogs pretended to mate, hunching themselves against each other, dust swirling and their feet spitting pebbles until a truck, rounding the bend, sounded the fruitful call.

It was, now, merely the onset of September, and if James Senior had not said when he would return to gather them together again—flowers bunched and, proffered, lovely—it did not seem to Rosette that it would be soon.

The Falls Church River swelled and on its top floated shoes and sometimes what looked like ribbons trailing from tin cans of couples having wed upstream. Once a wooden kitchen chair stuck at the mouth of the culvert. Fine drizzles began the mornings, fog came down from the mountains at night, and all the extra rooms were shut now against the damp. So, really, their dog had nowhere warm to be at night but between them on the rose-patterned rug, listening and, presumably, shoring up.

Years later, Rosette would have Claire's only child, Little Ben, they called him, with her for his amusement at a magic show. And, watching the magician scramble inverted china cups on a table (a girl in tights standing behind the magician, holding a poodle), she would think: *That* is how time feels—a panoply over the moving array. Sitting beside Little Ben, she held his hand, looking up and thinking, then looking down at his sweet head.

To brighten the house, Pauline began making forays on Saturdays into the attic where the owners, dead or living in Florida, stored all they had gathered from foreign travel, so, in this ministering to herself, their rooms took in vases from China—only this at first, though there were no flowers to put in them, the forsythia by the back steps stripped and scattered.

Afternoons, they would walk down the hill from the school, the dog romping before them, through the field where they had played at noon—even Pauline in her Red Cross shoes, a whistle dangling from a string on her dress—and past the dump wherein lay ice boxes, front seats of cars, the lace of scuppernongs. Then, past the flat-bed truck and into the house, Pauline would sit at the kitchen table, slide off her pumps, saying, "Well, Honey, another day," and sighing.

On the table would sit the extra pair of shoes, to be cleaned, and to Rosette, looking from the stove as she put on Pauline's tea water, it was a puzzle of sights: the blue and white checkered oil cloth of the table, the dark red shoes on which mud had dried, their two sets of books almost identical, Pauline's outstretched arm on which dangled the charm bracelet James Senior had given her, and the tall Chinese vase of brightest green and the tiniest flowers on a background of white.

Just off the edge of the table a thread from Pauline's sweater might sway in the air's movement of the dog settling at her feet. Behind her head the afternoon light coming through the half-curtained windows seemed to stop at the ladder-back chair. By now Pauline's eyes would be closed, her head resting on the chair's top slatting, her exposed throat pinkish.

Several times after they had written their letters to James Senior and to Claire, Pauline looked out the window and suggested they take the Greyhound to church in Harris. "It's not that far," she would add, for between them on the kitchen table would be James Senior's address as contrast, their two scripts seemingly doubling the miles to a N.Y.C. 49th Street.

But, they had been into Harris one Saturday for Pauline's outdoor shoes and had seen that Harris, too, was an outpost, nothing to recommend it now that Pauline had the shoes but this church they had only heard about. No dogs ran loose in Harris, but old men dozed on the benches in the square. One had awakened himself to whistle at Pauline.

Claire wrote to them on Irene's lavender note cards that Irene was taking her to the Modern Redeemer of the Young Nazarene Church on Saturday nights and that, any Saturday now, they would ask her to sing gospel in the choir. "We dress up," she added, and, on reading all of this, Pauline told Rosette that she had so much to say to Irene on a number of matters that she couldn't talk. So, shoving the letter over to Rosette, she called the dog and together they climbed the stairs to the attic as Rosette read.

Where was James Junior on Saturday nights? Now, a sequela, if Rosette forgot him, her temples stung, the stars seemed to puff and redden.

That night Pauline brought down a large fan, from India, she said, a *punkah*, she added, smiling; and around her neck hung a long silk scarf—"Japan *or* China," said Pauline, twirling it through her fingers. And, suddenly, Rosette knew that, even if allowed, *she* would not go to the attic.

After that, their rooms took on the shapes and colors of every place the owners had gone to, even Holland, the bathroom door propped open by a blue and yellow wooden shoe Pauline filled with pebbles from the drive.

Now after school Pauline rested her sore feet on a carved footstool around which circled miniature elephants. And on Sundays, Pauline unwrapped the silverware, handles made, she said, from the tusks of just such elephants.

"Do you think we should?" said Rosette. But Pauline said, "Them? They'll never be back, Honey. To this place?", which now was a carnival of sorts, Rosette's eyes jumping.

"Oh my God," said Pauline one morning, leaning over to shake Rosette's cot. "Look"—Pauline pointing down between them to the dog on whose red flanks the sun flared redder. "See there?"

But Rosette was looking at Pauline's left arm, at the swaying fringe of a robe Pauline had found in the attic, when Rosette had not known Pauline slept in their clothes. "Just old her," said Rosette. "I'm *sleepy,*" though she was not.

"Well we've been *blind,*" said Pauline, sliding out of bed and stooping by the dog. Rosette watched her cup her hands on the dog's side, the charm bracelet's little star and telephone receiver and gold cross tinkling as the dog hit her tail on the rug. "Can't you see?"

"Babies?" said Rosette, for the fur between Pauline's hands ballooned.

"Puppies. More than one *puppy,*" said Pauline. "How *could* she?" she asked, and, as she climbed back into bed: "*When,* I want to know."

Rosette watched Pauline close her eyes. She listened to the dog make a low sound James Senior would have understood; then the dog was quiet and Rosette, lying still, began thinking.

"Don't tell your father," said Pauline.

And it would be years before Rosette's vision would come: James Senior driving up and, after hugging them, calling the dog. Pauline would say, "She's in the house," after which nothing of lapsed time would come to Rosette's imagination but James Senior scooping up the tiny, slippery dogs into a grocery bag. Then she would be standing on the bank across from him and behind him Pauline would be crying as he said over and over, "Hush." Slowly and one by one he would drop them into the river. Their bodies would make the water ripple, one widening circle after another.

And it would be longer still before, envisioning this, Rosette would think to call out, "*Why* are you dropping them in one at a time?", the question itself, when it came, dropped into the sound of water, of Pauline's whimpering, and, then, of the outrageous quiet. James Senior would have performed this in his pin-striped suit.

Pauline filled their days of waiting with Saturday trips to Harris by Greyhound, the man at the A & P giving her bones for the dog, which she would unwrap and lay on the kitchen floor, saying, "From Frank," and, "Stupid dog," softly.

So the dog's fur shone and, added to their own sounds, the sound of gnawing.

"And don't tell Claire, who *would* tell your father," added Pauline one Sunday. Then Pauline laughed. "Do you remember," she asked, "when she named all her dolls after herself?"

Because of their trips into Harris, neither Rosette nor Pauline went now to the Post Office for stamps or to the Feed Store for salt or thread, the barking of the culprits, as Pauline called them, only a conglomerate sound from the hill where now bulldozers extended the by-pass. With the mongrel dogs there amidst the excitement, Pauline could *almost* forget, she said, they were ugly as sin. And, watching Pauline brush their dog's fur, Rosette imagined the puppies as full-grown, right front paws crooked, noses pointing skyward, the sound of James Senior's gun, and birds for each of them, falling.

One Saturday Pauline came down from the attic wearing a black velvet cape and, swirling around in the hall, she tucked Rosette under it, laughing. That day, in the cape, she took Rosette to the movie house in Harris—"Gene Tierney," whispered Pauline. "Your father met her once." And, after the movie, at Miseldine's, Frank sat with them while they drank hot chocolate, Pauline across from Rosette with the hood of the cape curving around her dark hair, Fat Frank by her, the two of them laughing, inventing names for the dogs. And at home that night, running through the drizzle from the side of the road where the bus had dropped them, Pauline noticed her own shape: "Look." And for Rosette she ballooned the cape, laughed, and pretended to bark.

Slowly, over an afternoon and an evening, they came, Pauline and Rosette following the sounds of whining coming from beneath the basement stairs. "Goodness, goodness," said Pauline, counting, getting up, even, from the dinner table to go down to count. "Eleven!" Pauline called—black, white, black-and-white spotted. Stubby tails. Then, a tiny gray one.

Now they walked to school without the dog, though Pauline told the children how many dogs they had now and how many the mother's little pouches of milk, even holding a contest for the naming of the littlest dog, whose eyes wouldn't open, no matter Pauline talked to it, saying, "Open your eyes, Little One," and, "Don't you want to see the world?", until Rosette found herself whispering, "Open up, open up."

Then Rosette was ill, so sick the county nurse came to quarantine the house with a sign she hung by the front steps which not even the postman used. Rosette in fever thought she heard James Senior talking, and Frank, saying he would go buy some Co-Cola. Once she opened her eyes to see that Pauline had moved her cot to the parlour and had built a fire of twigs in the grate. If she awoke during the night, she would see that Pauline slept on the rug beside her, but sometimes, looking down after the fire had died out, she would think it was the dog.

Once she woke to feel the littlest puppy moving beside her feet, and then in sleep she dreamed it was James Junior's tiny fists resting on one ankle. If she felt hot, Pauline fanned her with the *punkah,* saying, "Sleep, sleep."

The wind blowing the sign tacked by the door was, to Rosette, the birds returning.

When she was able to sit up and eat soup: the sight of Pauline's escorts, their dog and all the little ones like splotches around her feet, Pauling holding the bowl high in one hand and, in the other, the littlest dog, tucked next to her chest in the crook of her arm. "Funny!" said Pauline. "They're not even cute anymore," which Rosette could see was, by James Senior's standards, true.

"He didn't come while I was sick, did he," she asked.

"Well no," said Pauline. "Lord, I'd have had to *hide* them, so thank goodness. Now eat up," by which, Pauline explained, she would get strong enough to help her figure out what to do with the dogs.

"Do you know," Rosette will say to her husband years later, when Rosette is verging still on absolute wakefulness or, as the case may be, beginning the waking-sleep, "after we grew up, every dog Pauline got *died* on her?"

Recovering, Rosette stayed in the house, her books spread on the table, the dog under the table by her feet, the little ones running through the hall and kitchen or dropping almost together beside Rosette's chair to sleep before beginning again. From the window, Rosette could watch Pauline winding down the path from school. Always now Pauline wore the cape, the books she held under it a bundle, and, if it were cold, Rosette could see one of Pauline's hands sticking out to hold the hood close to her face. When she came onto the steps, the dogs ran to her noise, began their barking, high-pitched. "Oh, hush," Pauline would call, going past them to feel Rosette's forehead. "We've *got* to do something."

Then one day Pauline began bringing from the dump bits of wire and old boards, Rosette watching her deposit the junk in a clear spot by the flat-bed truck. "We'll build a pen," said Pauline, puffing, her hands red from rust, rust powdery on the books she dropped on the table. And from the attic Pauline brought down crates and an old Army knapsack for her books, which she began to wear beneath the cape, a mound, both hands full as she began dragging from the dump parts of cars, an icebox door.

She asked one evening as they ate supper, "And where is your father when I need him?", forgetful, Rosette could see, though when

86

they wrote to him they never forgot. "I am well and fine," Rosette wrote. "Momma too."

Then Rosette was well and together they went to the Feed Store, buying bags of dry food for the dogs. While she had been abed, they had finished the by-pass, the air quiet now but for the trucks, the barking of the dogs which had come again to sleep and to play around the Post Office and the Feed Store.

If a dog crossed in front of Pauline, she kicked out, saying, "Go on, go on, you've done enough," and, turning to Rosette: "Wouldn't you say?" And, after buying stamps: "Your sister hardly writes us anymore, you know," about whom, since the time James Junior had settled at her feet, Rosette had hardly thought.

"Well it's true," said Pauline. "And when she does write, there's no *information* in them, so I don't know," Pauline's voice trailing off.

And now they did not go into Harris, Pauline saying they hadn't time.

The dogs, knocking against the tables, broke all the vases one by one.

Pauline built the dog pen alone, Rosette watching from the kitchen as Pauline twisted together with bits of wire the pieces of wood and metal and old doors. On her cuts, she poured iodine, Rosette watching, Pauline shutting her eyes, the stain making Pauline say as she sat down to eat, "I'm not hungry. Who *could* be?", dropping her hands into her lap.

"I could help," said Rosette.

"Help?" said Pauline. "Help! God help us, you can't help. Now eat." So Rosette ate, the food knotting in her stomach, Pauline, she imagined, growing thin in front of her.

On the day Pauline carried all the dogs to the pen, even their own, it rained and, still, from all over the county, as Pauline said, the mongrels came, to run, barking, around the pen, their own dog leaping and snarling against the wire or the boards.

Later, from inside the house, Pauline watched, her hair still wet from her bath, the fringed robe, Rosette noticed, sticking to her legs. She was barefoot, the house quiet, as if pressed upon from the dogs' barking outside. "We'll place an ad in the Harris paper," she said. "But who'd have them?"

Then Pauline was running out the door, down the steps, through the dogs and into the pen where, Rosette saw, she scooped up the little gray dog and, holding it close to her, her robe flapping around her legs, ran back into the kitchen with it. "For Frank," she told Rosette. "We'll fatten him up and give him to Frank."

In time James Senior did return to find them just as, he imagined, he had left them, driving up with Claire in the car, her almost-white hair curled into tight bunches and, resting inside one curl, a grosgrain ribbon of bright red, a phase, he must have thought, she was going through.

He will stoop and pat the dog, saying they not only have to pack up but get some meat on the dog if she's going to be of any use at all. And he will take them off to California before he drifts off altogether, taking the dog, only Rosette knowing where to and precisely on what day the dog fell over and died.

And though they have Claire with them a few years before she, too, goes off, it is always as if they were still adjusting to her, the curls, which Pauline says are so pretty, which she touches now and then on passing by Claire, in fact become for Pauline that which divides time — *when* she lost this daughter who turned mostly silent.

In time Pauline lets a man like Frank court her, though nothing much, she tells Rosette by phone, is bound to come of it. And she begins to try keeping a dog in the house as protection against the changing times.

Rosette marries and — this respite — for a long time does not daydream.

However, just after Pauline has awakened from a nap and has come into the kitchen, she kneels down at the doorway to pat the dog they have begun to call Frank. Rosette is studying at the table, almost asleep herself. She turns to watch Pauline rub the dog, who, over time, has chewed off the design of elephants on Pauline's footstool, who begins now to chew on Pauline's robe.

"Stop it," says Pauline, hitting out at the dog. And then the dog bites her: Pauline rising, Pauline at the sink, the water splashing, Pauline's hands shaking, Pauline crying. . . .

And that night she throws Frank into the pen with the others, saying as she comes in, "I can't take it, I can't take it."

And always they sleep to the sound of barking.

Finally, early one morning before school (although, as it turns out, they do not go to school on this morning), Rosette watches Pauline carrying out the bag of food to the pen, her kicking out at the mongrels who roam around the pen, then watches Pauline opening the pen door and squeezing past the dogs trying to get out and those trying to get in. The bag is held high over Pauline's head, the dogs, even theirs, jumping, the gate catching on Pauline's shoes, and then the mongrel dogs pushing behind Pauline into the pen. Pauline is standing in the middle of the pen as the dogs jump and, as if in slow-motion, the bag falls, Pauline is falling, Pauline is scrambling up with the dogs all over her.

It seems to Rosette that Pauline turns on her side purposely to face her as the dogs jump on her one last time before running from the pen. Pauline raises herself half-way, looks at Rosette through the window, she opens her mouth, and out, like an endless white string, comes a sound high-pitched, looping.

Years later, when Rosette's husband's mother dies, Rosette will stand before the open coffin for a long time, explaining that it is, really, her first view of death.

And when her husband wakes her from the swirling of her teeth grinding in sleep, she almost mentions her dreaming, saying to herself that she would but for his mother—a politeness, she thinks, except that the dream, slowly and like a season approaching, moves into the hours of waking and appropriates its own time.

Rosette walks with Little Ben down the dirt road by the Falls Church River, in summer, the last August heat making the air still. Little Ben, who has never grown, holds her hand, his white hair even with her elbow. Above them the telephone lines swoop low, the sky is pink. Claire is down the road at the house, spreading over a long, carved table the white cloth on the top of which she will put sweet potato pies and platters of chicken wings, crescent rolls and honey.

Little Ben and Rosette do not talk; they swing their arms and almost hum. The spire of the little country church picks up the last light and appears pinkish against the graying sky. Then, slowly and in the straightest line comes the black cortege, James Senior's black-painted Nash Ambassador leading, inside of which sit his other wives and his other children, all Rosette's age when she was Little Ben's size. They wave from the lowered windows. James Senior tips his hat. Frank, on his motorcycle, rides amongst the yellow of forsythia tied to the handlebars.

And then, drawn by dogs grown sleek and deepest red, with long tails held straight and feathery, comes the flat-bed truck on which Pauline rides, the tiny gray dog perched near her, not barking.

Rosette squeezes Little Ben's hand, the crows, keeping up, swooping to perch on the telephone wires above them, "the only ones," Rosette tells Little Ben, "uninvited."

Setting

Claire's long legs: scissors above which her body puffed. When she leaned over in the rented nurse's uniform, the rose of nylon panties showing through, her red mane disappeared, its mingling gray, down to where Patrick-Marion lay on the camelia-white of the almost-dead. I thought, then, she was herself going to seed. One tiny breath of air and a thousand black-tipped shoots of silk would fall about him like a waterless snow.

But I would not breathe. Most of the hair gone from his head, the brows a little dusting of sand, eyes the color of rabbits' and, below this, the green baize coverlet folded double. The sight: as if a magician had been caught unaware with his wares ajumble. Had thrown a cloth over his accoutrements of delight, which is to say I loved Patrick-Marion as he had been.

Life partitioned, I thought, looking at them, all of glowing Korea having waned to this tiny spot of grass where Claire received the ambulance and him. Seen like that, her strands of gray were wire or harp string.

"Isn't this just what I predicted?" she hissed, ending the metal procession down the rise, past my humming car. She tapped her painted nails on the car door, after which I rolled up the window and drove, down around the mills and their villages squatting in the falling dark, and up to farmland where, under stars, Charlie paced with his cows.

"She has him now," I said, "which is all we can do," when, of course, we had done nothing, as Claire, had she been with us, would have mentioned. The billowing with flowers down hospital halls, it is true, was nothing.

I listened to Charlie sigh; had there been a salt lick near, he would have pressed his tongue to it. Marion would by now be on the

91

daybed, Claire's hands in his. We were out with the stars.

So I tucked Charlie into bed, in the room where his wife's brushes and combs lay aligned as they had always lain, to keep him company, he said. Her hair had been beautiful and long; for her death, they had braided it.

I drove straight home, almost happy, for which I was ashamed. As if the Red Sea had parted, bodies walled up on either side, how could I not smile, favored to be among those walking through? I curled next to Richard's back and, from that vantage point, I lay in wait.

For days my arms ached, as if I had carried Marion, and in my sleep lights flashed off and on, little matches, three-on-one, my hands in Richard's, cupped.

If, any Sunday, we drove down Route 14 and took the proper "Y," rose with the hills up to Tugaloo Road by 11:00, we could stand in the back of the tiny white church and observe Claire at the front pew, her right hand resting on his metal chair, the left holding the hymnal just above his head, which hung to one side on the canvas. And, later, observe the bustle of getting him down the twelve steps onto packed clay again. Claire, all business and sunshine. I would have sworn she had been born to tend, had I not remembered our mother's languishing. *Now* she was not skittish. And they loved her, the minister and his choir singing to her burden and to his, if he could think, which no one knew, his head like a daffodil's after rain.

Ladies in dresses and gloves reached out to pull his blanket straight; Claire shook her head, "No," in that reserve of her knowledge. Only she touched him. Charlie would put one hand on the arm support, lean close, look.

On the steps, we shivered, winter rain or clear skies; and when it rained, Claire held above their heads her beige raincoat and, all about her, was the bobbing undersky of black umbrellas.

"Let's go eat some dinner," I would say those first few weeks, seating Charlie between us in Richard's truck, to bolster him, I thought. And Richard, then, would have to reach across the back of the seat to touch me, and Charlie, I noticed, turned to look past me

92

to the scenery, to the birds swooping down to feed, to the clouds turning almond-colored with winter.

"I don't know," Charlie would say to the birds or the clouds, voice dipping at my ear as if itself ravenous.

Then I gave Charlie the place by the door. Even in the cold he rolled down the window and hung one arm out. Except at the curves, I put Richard's right hand on my thigh.

We would have been eating long before Claire had lifted Patrick-Marion down to his bed, even though the fast-food idea had not come to fruition. It must have been, with time, that the mobile boys home from Korea could not, life or death, wait to consume. Some entrepreneur would notice by and by.

Full and sleepy, we would drive Charlie, full and sleepy, home. And, I thought once, how the waitress at McCoy's had no idea from whence we came. She thought we were happy regulars; in time she found herself able to leave the orange slices off the sides of our plates. What did Marion eat?

I had seen in the church parking lot two ladies try to press on Claire food, Tupperwares of Royal jello with fruit, another of fried chicken wings. Claire rolled her eyes; the ladies looked down. Oh, she was making his dying a formal thing! No half maraschinos, peach cubes, or the salty wings of the home-raised bird. Claire made their faces freeze, as, I see now, she wanted. For an instant, she frightened me. I wanted our mother back, and saw her in that same instant unshrouded, trying on a Sunday to read, lifting one hand from where she sat with a book to swat Claire on the legs. We needed her now.

On the grayish days, as Richard worked, I stood often at the windows, thinking, I suppose, or trying to talk, as when children string together empty evaporated milk cans, hide behind trees, and whisper because it is unfair to the science of string and can to shout. Thus we were by hope and flimsiness connected—me, Richard at work on the old Buick, Claire, our mother resting, Charlie and his restless son. At such games, children give up at twilight, nature and not themselves closing down for the day. Then, inside, the houses seem especially warm, the lights are brighter than they will seem again. Richard, coming home, was heat and light. I snuggled in, and did not ask who held Claire close.

It was she, I think now, our mother wanted close, that, instead, they had made a wordless pact since there was nothing left between them but the letting loose. In winter, birds fly south, we think to feast, but is it so?

Claire would have let us visit, any day. For propriety, I imagined that first day, I had Charlie go in alone. I waited sitting on the steps, hands folded as if gloves in my lap. And it was, I think, the only time Charlie cried. He was with them for a long time—the sky changed, the wind died down. The folds of his skin were wet as he stepped out.

After that, we brought gifts to the door, Claire's door which, after Marion came, she painted red, color of church doors behind which she had once played the organ.

It was a slow build-up, the tambourine-rattle of our shopping trips, Saturdays, when Charlie could get the colored boys to tend the cows. So we would leave with Reese and Rodney waving, red bandanas tied to their throats as if to make their eyes stand out. We waved, settled in for the drive. Richard did not go; he relinquished me and slept. On Main Street we took it slow, meandering especially in the five-and-dime: after-shave, long woolen scarves, underwear. We touched all they had for men such as Patrick-Marion had been. The clerks hovered—oh, had we told them what we really wanted, we could have made them sick, how the honed description is pulled like a tooth from desire.

It was there I saw the drinking glass filled with glass straws, crooked at the ends. Up the aisle, Charlie unfurled a child's flag, waved it. His work boots on the wooden floor seemed to singe the air; I knew what lovely Patrick-Marion ate and did not eat.

We bought him nothing. We sat over sandwiches at the cafe and looked away.

We tried the movies, Hopalong Cassidy, the choking dust, the horse, while Charlie slumped beside me, sleeping, his head thrown back, popcorn falling from the box on his knees. He would not waken even when the lights came on. I leaned close to shake him, and he woke to kiss my eyebrows once.

And so it was after those first silly trips to town that we got serious. Inspired, I think, for when we thought of it together, in the market which delivered Claire's food, we were idling in the soup aisle: black bean with sherry, real turtle, red and white bisques, a promise of Spain on the can with the dancing girl. I looked at Charlie, who shrugged, Why not?

And so, at first, we had them include in her box of necessaries the exotic can or box of wafers or cheese from Ireland. Toffees once. It made Charlie smile, and then he tired of it. *I* tired of imagining Claire opening the box, saying, "I swan," or, "What in the world does he think he's doing?"

Did she talk to Patrick-Marion? Hum to him as he slept?

One night I dreamed that, long after he died, Claire sent to me by mail a lined sheet of paper on which was written

I have no regrets,
Patrick-Marion

when, as we all knew, he could not hold a pen.

After the food, we sent new uniforms, the modern kind in shades of Easter eggs or mints. On the left-hand pocket of a pink one, Charlie had her name embroidered. But she sent them back. I saw on a stack of merchandise marked down for sale her name in red. And, even at the church, she wore the dingy rented uniform—sometimes we saw it dipping down beneath her winter coat as she leaned to straighten Patrick-Marion in his chair.

Her hair was braided now, a coil of several braids pinned up in the back. She smiled less, her face seeming especially white against the black of her coat. Even at Christmas she went unadorned, when all the ladies wore pins of holly. His lap robe was navy, nothing showing above it but the face we were not accustomed to.

For a time we stayed home, or, rather, in both our homes, for we went to Charlie's house on the coldest nights. Richard brought in fire wood and, as I cleaned, they played checkers or sat, simply, looking into the fire.

Sometimes I stopped at a doorway to look at Richard, imagining someone close to him dying—what shape, then, would he assume? I cooked, filling the Cold Spot with casseroles.

Looking at Charlie from the door as we left, I felt my forehead burn, where he had kissed me.

"He'll last," said Richard, "as long as Patrick-Marion lasts."

Turning in the car, we looked at the little house, seemingly smaller in the barn's shadow falling across the roof. The moon hung frozen in the sky; it seemed time should stop, that it and the porch light should become in that instant a burning too.

In the month of January, Charlie bought Claire brooches, at Leffel's near the Post Office, where he had so often gone to talk after reading Marion's letters from the Front. Now he and Leffel had no need to talk. Leffel spread the imitation gold and cut-glass brooches across a velvet cloth. I stood aside: *their* sense of taste, not mine or Claire's. We were our mother's children; in times of trouble, I thought, becoming anything; in others, impeccable, and quiet.

Charlie had them boxed, with ribbon, and I waited in the car as he walked down the rise to her door. He held the boxes behind his back, a suitor.

And, of course, in time, Charlie died, after Patrick-Marion died, just as Richard promised. Then Claire cleaned her little house of all the glass straws, lap robes, and rows of canned goods too foreign to eat. She shook her hair down. With it like that, flowing, she came to see Charlie put beside Marion, who rested beside his mother. Nothing to say; the choir sang to them all, including Claire. After that, she moved away, with a man who had come to sell her a portable organ. I hear from her now and then, her voice quiet, suggesting she sits by the phone in a dress of navy wool, with pearls at its neck. In the background sometimes is the sound of artificial music, of which anyone else would ask, How can she stand it?

"She's got enough jewelry," Leffel said one day. "I think she probably needs a dress, something fancy, what with winter." And so we were off buying lapelled dresses, or dresses with shawl collars. Colors too bright, "for winter," Charlie told the saleswoman. Then a full slip of deepest purple. It made him smile: the ladies swishing night-time fabric before him, his head cocked to one side.

As a child, Claire's legs dangled from the piano bench, her sashes hanging below the seat, shoe buckles hitting the wood of the bench.

The stockings he bought were black, with diamond-shapes woven at the ankles. A satin handbag, with sequins. Lipsticks, little tins of powder, perfume marked Made in Paris in tiny chamois bags tied with string ties. As we walked to the car, each filigree ribbon seemed to freeze, and from the distance even of the car as Charlie stood on her stoop, I saw that he shivered.

"Make him stop," I asked Richard. But Richard said to let him be. All of us were waiting, hot and cold in turn.

We did not see Patrick-Marion again. On his last day, Claire had the ambulance return. We sat with Charlie in the days that followed. Claire did not insist, and Charlie said he would rather not look. "Of course," I said, Richard nodding, a long-held breath seeming to loosen from him, for Charlie's sake. We invent as we go along.

Claire came to the service in the swishing dress of royal blue, purple slip showing, her lips the brightest fuchsia, brooches glittering all down her front, seams straight on the black, diamond-patterned hose. Rouge was on her cheek-bones, her forehead, a dusting across her nose. Her coat was flung carelessly across one arm, the sequined hand bag barely visible. Little curls slipped from the braided coil, and in its center sat an emerald brooch. Her nails were red.

We did not at first recognize her. We held our breaths and for a long time, it seemed, we thought.

Then she walked toward us, this picture of love and perfect fury, which most of us will never know.

The Musician

I was learning from Juanita what death, or music meant.

She came in dreams not initially to participate but to stand, a coalescence, at the edge of rooms barn-sized, open on two sides, weeds growing to the floor boards. Her shoes made wickets in the grass; between them, mounds, child-length.

Outside, it was bright—afternoon sun, the last of definite energy; it hurt the eyes. Once she stepped forward and displayed her teeth. She flung her head back as I said that I liked them—artificial, even, star-colored. "Oh," she said, "I don't at all," her head seeming to toss involuntarily so that I could observe too its whiteness at the scalp, the blending of hair and scalp by whiteness.

Or, asserting herself, she touched one arm, pulling me gently to her, to whisper, "You can't serve that cake. If you'll travel to Faulkner's hometown, to the museum there, you'll see his mother served a cake like that once."

Luigi was at the sink, saying as he washed his hands, that he would buy champagne. He smiled, the water splashed, arcs of light scattering as the droplets fell.

The cake was two-tiered, of rectangles stacked one upon another, jutting this way and that as if to resemble a hot-climate palace. It was covered with white frosting which gleamed as egg-shells sometimes do, or pearls. It sat on a long table, on cardboard, ready for cutting: and, beside it, Juanita sneered.

Moreover, one early morning when the birds still slept, Juanita took my grandmother's place, crouched inside a cupboard, at the farm, on a Saturday night. She waited immobile until my father tried to tiptoe in, the moon head-sized behind his head as the door opened. And, springing out, Juanita beat him with a broom—my father, who had not yet married her, ruined her, tossed her sideways, who wanted in the time of this dream merely not to become a Holy Roller, which keeping of his body off church floors and his writhing at least upright took him, as it turned out, a long, long way. But in this version of his youth, Juanita, grown big with age and sipping wine and eating food quickly, swatted his little limping body as it wended its way out. The screen door slammed.

Of course Juanita telephoned: my waking life. We had ordinary conversations which were too real, air bubbling from the hooked fishes' mouths. In sleep, not hours before, I would have felt my teeth loosen, as if a tongue could pour!, fall on the pillow—pearls beneath a goose's belly. Luigi would find them, scoop them up for safe-keeping.

What makes the world painful? Objects, including the sight of bodies. Cake. When Luigi married me, we served the most beautiful *petit-fours*, roses set on their tops, sweet and lemony, tiny leaves beside them, touching. The minister's robe was the lavender that brides' mothers wear, or girls barely old enough to walk at Eastertime, who lock their baskets in their fists.

He sweated, this minister. His hands shook, his eyes looked shy. And all the while Luigi smiled at me so wide a smile I knew not to turn to stone.

Mornings, straddling me after I curve one arm around his black curls, Luigi says, "You called?" In half-sleep, I smile. He, then, with a toss of his head, sends Juanita packing, her skirts aswish in the long grass, soft light shining on her head, and, seen leaving, her face turned to the other side, she is lovely and, imagine, graceful.

Once, just as Luigi entered me, I noticed Juanita had walked to my father's door. One ravaged hand raised to knock; she knew *he* would have to answer.

"You like?", Luigi always asked me once inside me.

I didn't run to the back of my father's house to warn him. His window was open and near the ground. I could have leaned in, called. But he had turned down the page of his book, one ear-piece of his bi-focals dangled from his teeth. So I let him get up from the chair, *see* who was at the door.

100

Luigi, did you know what you were doing? Did our minister wear such a robe to dazzle you? Each anniversary I will send him a note, violets sprayed across it.

But, also, Luigi has a child he's never seen, nor I, though I had shown him *my* child, Paul, the boy almost-grown. Often, then, I asked Luigi, "How old is she, did you say?"

"*Him*," Luigi would answer. "A boy, age two."

Her, I had met, the mother—sweet, as a method, and thin, and incapable, the baby invisible under her skirt. In time, we had heard it had arrived, and we did not travel to see it.

"Yes," I said to Luigi. "A boy. I simply forgot."

Me and Luigi? Lightning split a blue spruce pine and from its rings our grandmothers, having met by accident, emerged together, holding us. Before we slept at night or when we traveled to the store for groceries, I sang to Luigi songs such as grandmothers know, by which Luigi seemed older.

And my father had had a child by his last wife, copies of whose pictures he sent by mail. Luigi and I said as we looked at them together that she was beautiful, all, I think, my father got from this girl, our words, over her pictures, which words we remembered to restate in our letters to him. He lived alone, he had pictures, yellowed, Juanita's face and body cut from them. "Is that you?", Luigi asked. "That's very sweet."

Thus, we too had pictures everywhere, none, of course, of Luigi's boy. And none, either, of the boy whose twin I had been. On some days I reasoned that Juanita had gone knocking on my father's door to ask for pictures of him—perfect child, Juanita had said, simply without breath, or, as I saw it, a fish contented.

When autumn came, Luigi polished the car, washed its windows, moving then to the house and its windows, the porch, the porch swing,

101

all clean for my exit, our going and returning, should I feel like it. "You may want to take a trip," said Luigi. "So the car's all set, if we want," how, you see, Luigi talked—*you, me*. Language wedded to his body, for Luigi worked with his hands—cars, loose copper drain pipes, broken steps, anything our neighbors wanted. And if it was odd to them that Luigi loved music, simply they didn't know from whence he came. In death, stretched out, his mother wore a look of such repose it put a shame in all the mourners, as if they could not move smoothly. Her look was for having made Luigi. Of course she rested satisfied, I say.

Often and at times without pattern, I thought how Paul's father and I never saw Paul together, never, say, Paul on one side of a room, us on another. I was sure this absence changed the manner in which Paul stood, how he held his head, changed even the air in which he stood.

The days were still hot. "If we take a trip," I said to Luigi, "let's wait until this Indian Summer passes," when, I thought, I might be done with over-sleeping, "the bride's rest," Luigi's cousins called it, not knowing Juanita flitted behind the fence posts, the old well. Nor looking really, at my face, neither young nor old, rather, poised, *my* ornamental cousin Garcia Lorca, who said, "We will nail up the windows and the rain and the long nights will crawl in over the bitter grasses."

Present in mind at Luigi's mother's mourning scene were only, I think, Luigi and his mother. They seemed lonely. Then Luigi turned to me.

Not minding the heat, Luigi's friends or a cousin or two came by in the evening to visit. They loosened their boots and propped their feet on the porch railing and, leaning back, Luigi's beer in hand, they talked, their voices drifting in to me where I lay on the bed, "the weather," Luigi would explain. Or from where I sat reading, I would watch them repair one of their cars. Before settling down, I would fix sandwiches and, always, Luigi found a way to kiss me privately. He would choose as the place an ear or the inside of one arm.

One afternoon, they oiled the porch swing so that, afterwards, when I knew Juanita took her place on it as Luigi and I sat together in the kitchen, I would remember, later as I dreamed, only the sound of her feet on the gray-painted wood. Swish, swish, as if she were a child. Her feet, in reality, were long and bony. Were she to have lived six years more, the doctors might have operated to remove the jutting bone. Luigi's mother's feet were, of course, hidden by flowers and a short, yellow coverlet on top of which her arms rested.

In the south, distances seem farther between towns than in other places, except perhaps in Russian novels, in snow. In truth, Luigi and I could have visited Juanita every week. "Just say when, Sweets," Luigi had said.

However, it was as if I had counted every tree between Juanita's house and ours, had seen her red cape flare behind each one as she came inching forward.

Luigi was, I think now, waiting on me, the minister's eyes shy, I suppose, with knowledge beyond us on our Day of Days, the pronouncing of a state, he must have guessed, not rendering it so.

Luigi said he would learn to cook. He said it must be similar to learning how an engine works. I sat by the kitchen window, cooling, watching, Luigi so beautiful. Once I thought I heard Juanita laughing in delight, an apothegm of sorts.

The food was lovely too—baked fish sprinkled with paprika, a billow of white sauce around it. And asparagus. Pots and pans everywhere, Luigi sweating. . . .

We were getting Luigi's mother accustomed to me when she died. I had come to sleep pristine on the single bed downstairs. Hearing Luigi as he stooped down to tell me, I had tried to scramble inside a wall, a corner, pale yellow. Time does not flow.

"Luigi," I said, "let's ask Paul to come visit us."

"Well sure," said Luigi. "Here, taste this." And I did, smiling.

Instead, Juanita called. "I'm sick," she said, "I'm not kidding this time."

"All this?", Luigi asked, looking at what I had packed and placed by the door to take. Luigi's records, the old violin he had said he wanted to learn to play, my books, Luigi's huge yellow rain-slicker, his favorite roasting pan. The car was full, the house closed up tight. As we drove, I rested my head on Luigi's shoulder, and it seemed sometimes, at the curves, that Juanita sat beside the door. "Maybe Paul can come there," I said.

We found her as I had imagined we would, when the clomp, clomping of her red shoes would stop, the door left cracked open for us, behind us the late sun and inside the green coolness of her walls and the drawn curtains, her body looking longer yet on the brocade sofa, her shoes off, one arm across her stomach, the other on a cushion, palm-up, the head thrown back and, as we pushed open the door, the color white, of hair and face and, for that instant in which her eyes focused on us, the variegated white of her eyes. We dropped our bundles and went forward, both of us crouching by her, me closest to her face. "What's wrong, Momma?", I whispered.

"You think they *know*?" she said, sitting up, fluffy hair sprayed across her forehead. "Luigi," she said, brushing one hand across his knee, "would *you* think they know?" She slapped his knee. "No! They don't."

"Should we bring the rest of our things in, Momma?", I asked her, softly still, which was how I talked to her, always, as if the modulated voice would make my body patient.

"Well sure!" said Juanita. "Now let me look at you, Luigi," and she stood up, pulling Luigi with her, to turn him around before her. She was his height; he smiled, smiling still and turning as I went to get our things.

Luigi cooked in the tiny kitchen, doorless, by which Juanita was able to watch as she lay on the couch—the refrigerator door opening,

104

shutting, Luigi pulling out a stool to place a pan on, the windows being flung open, one of Juanita's pink rollers falling from a sill onto the floor, Luigi calling out, "Hungry, you two?"

That first night, Juanita ate a tremendous amount. As I bent to kiss her, I noticed she smelled of spaghetti, that the couch had a stain where she had put her plate. "I like Luigi," she said. And I pulled the quilt close around her neck, I settled her in.

Outside our window, a wind stirred the oak tree. It was as if we were hemmed in. I raised myself on an elbow and I looked down at Luigi, almost sleeping. "Think," I said, "of how much she *ate*. I really have my doubts. . . ."

"No, no," said Luigi, pulling me close, "get some sleep. She knows something we don't know."

That night, of course, Juanita did not come sneaking through the grass. She was where she was—sleeping on the couch in her own house, her trees brushing at the windows and, under our bed, her shoes in neat little rows.

I think of those days as pewter-colored, though for a long time there was the brightest sun—we watered the willow in the yard and we sprayed down the dirt in the drive. Luigi replaced the screens on all the windows, cut the vines from the carport. I would not leave his side, and so we both browned, by which Juanita seemed, in contrast, whiter.

One day I drove alone to my father's house, and I cleaned it. I took his arm and we walked his property, past the old house Juanita had crouched in, running him off with her broom. The back door hung open and you could see from the road the little cupboard, too small for any human body. He asked, looking at my bare arm, if I needed a watch, and, days later, in the mail, to Juanita's house, came a silver watch, which I hid from Juanita.

The nights, now, were chilly; we closed all the windows, clear before Luigi's new screening. The sky turned gray and the color, I

105

thought, went with Luigi's music. Juanita hummed along, lifting her eyes now and then to flirt with Luigi, a smile, barely apparent, at her lips, which she still painted red. One night she gave him her violin bow. But Luigi couldn't play and Juanita said she was too tired to teach him now. "You should have," she said to me, "kept up with the violin."

For reasons I did not understand, Luigi and I did not put away anything we used, nor the violin case from which Juanita had taken the bow. So it sat on the green carpet, by the sofa, open, the three-legged tray sitting over it, and, on the tray, Juanita's glass of bicarbonate of soda and water.

"We can't possibly have Paul come here," I said to Luigi, looking around.

"Well sure we can," said Luigi. But, instead, I thought of Paul bringing to our door a girl, saying, "This is my girl." And, after we had met her, he would send pictures of the two of them, in a park, taken by a passer-by.

Juanita didn't know of my father's other wives—why should she?, I had thought. But, then, too she never spoke of him. We brought her magazines and, looking them over, she had Luigi change the furniture around. The couch, then, faced the windows, and, when Luigi and I came down the rise after going to the store, we would see, if the curtains were parted, Juanita waiting. Her head up and, I saw, glowing.

"Don't worry," said Luigi when I tossed at night. "One of the neighbors is watering the plants. It'll all be fine."

I think Luigi was happy. And there was so much for him to do. Take Juanita for little walks, for instance, the doctors shaking their heads and saying a little walk might help. I watched them from Juanita's place on the couch. His black head, hers white, bobbing over the rise and down, until there was nothing but quiet in her tiny house. What does she say to him?

I thought he was forgetting his own mother, his stooping on the floor beside her, one hand at her collarbone, only the pulse missing.

106

One morning, Luigi pulling me atop of him, I stopped over him as a sea-gull sometimes will over water. "Do you think," I whispered, "she *hears* us?", which thinking of had made me sick.

"Oh no," said Luigi, "she doesn't hear that well now, I've noticed," which, I think, was why I came to notice Juanita's watching me. I thought, as I passed her by or brought her a glass or an ashtray, of the sound in seashells, of the person holding one to an ear. He squints his eyes, he places himself imaginatively on a beach. He tilts his head.

No, Juanita did not die then; in fact, she lasted five years more, and, the last year, we brought her to our house, mine and Luigi's, so that she could have space around her, light and our trees and the sound under the trees of Luigi and his friends, pounding on something, or laughing. And Paul, in and out with each new girl, until he settled. Once, in that time, I met Luigi's boy, a formal loving-at-first-sight. And Luigi stayed the same. Anyone would love Luigi, and I have clung. Learning does not take memory away, which is what shells whisper.

I would be reading in the Queen Anne's chair, my legs out before me on the hassock. Luigi might be out with trash, trying to get it to burn even as a light rain fell. I would turn a page and be thinking of how he looked—yellow and shiny in the coat, the charcoal of its inside surface turned up at the sleeves, Luigi whistling. Then I would notice: Juanita watching me.

Or Luigi would hand me a platter across the table. I would be lifting one hand from my lap to receive it when, suddenly, it would seem so quiet that we both would look at Juanita, is she all right? She would have been watching me.

I thought, some nights, Luigi's hand resting on my back as he slept, that she was jealous, Luigi, at peace, just so. Alone, I decided, I will gather up her shoes from under the bed, when the time comes. I won't, I thought, let Luigi see them.

Then, one night when the rain shook the windows, driven hard against them by a wind, the lights flashing off twice and the house seeming to shake away from the cement slab holding it down, I rested my book in my lap, I turned it over, and I looked up, to Luigi stretched on the floor by Juanita's couch. *Luigi,* I thought smiling, though he did not see me, his head resting on an outstretched arm, turned toward the windows, toward the skirt of Juanita's couch. It could have been the only time Luigi was not facing me.

So—which I say almost smiling now—there was nowhere to look but at Juanita. She looked at me for a long time. The wind died down, it grew still outside and, inside, stiller yet.

Juanita's eyes narrowed, she tilted her head, as if listening. And I think it was this stillness she had waited so long for. And, on this night, her lips were dry, colorless, her hair uncurled, flat on her head.

I thought how far away Luigi was, as though there were miles of water between us. I saw it sparkling, without my looking down.

She raised one hand, which pointed at me. "You," she said, "have done me an injustice."

It was then, I think, after the air had fallen, as Luigi rose, came walking toward me, that I married him, in sickness and in health.

And Juanita, as we know, went on living.

Chanticleer

"all that vulgar beauty. . . ."
Elizabeth Bishop

Five years after the fact of death, the contents, *pasticcio*, surrounded them, their Papa's house — two rooms without electricity but a dozen windows, fireplace large enough to hold a roasting pig. And, outside, past Josie's slinky body framed in the door's screening, was, as they say, a buttermilk sky which would soon tinge, color of her hair, or Claire's, or Lucy's. Claire, the former beauty, kicked softly at a box which contained, so far, a dictionary. "What we need," she said, "is to write them all a letter."

"Who *to?*" said Josie, to the sky, to her pink-painted van parked by a clay bank, to his gardenia bush gone to seed. In her back pocket was a leather-bound pad for taking notes. Josie knew, for instance, who sent Christmas cards on time or late.

No, even in that aperçu of twilight they didn't want to begin the clean-up; Lucy didn't want to feel wistful, as when she sometimes says to Quentin, "I wish I'd learned to waltz." Always he says they can learn if they really want to, can get *some*body to give them the floor — how Quentin is: first you ask, *then* you let what you can't have sink in, except when Lucy imagines her lilac dress twirling, it's in another century: velvet ribbons, French doors, her eyes closed.

Still, they had eventually dressed for the clean-up — Claire in her black ballerinas, Josie in the taupe, as she called it, silk pants.

But heat weighed their muscles. Of the letter Claire said they ought to write, they thought, *Who to?* Or, maybe, Lucy thought, their memories were like a swept farm yard one fraction before dawn, not a feather stirring. All the while, Jim's cars tilted deeper into rust, any one of which could have held a coterie. Papa-the-bon-

109

vivant, Lucy said to herself, who came into full bloom after he left us, or, as he would have said, after he left "your mother," her name afterwards always strange—"And how is Pauline?"—until it seemed she, too, was one of the ladies he'd driven around to see the American sights. Pauline cast off, Lucy thought, joined him. It happened in the quiet.

"What we *need*," said Josie, "is some lemonade," and, as the screen door slammed behind her, Lucy watched Claire's eyes narrow.

"He shoulda died in November. It's cooler then."

In the South, pines rarely dip with snow. One Christmas Jim and Lucy had walked his property coatless, past *his* father's house sinking back into the ground and past each bush Jim had planted, flowering bushes so that in spring he could float a dozen single blossoms on every table and sill. The little touch.

"He did," Lucy reminded Claire. "You all just didn't come."

Nathan had come, albeit in Jim's third wife's belly, his being there why Lucy recently held him close, told him how it happened that Claire got fat. "Puffed up with fury," she told him. And Nathan squinched up his sun-burned nose; Lucy watched him think, his blond head dipping down.

"I know that, you shit," said Claire.

Then they were quiet for a minute, after which, as if a benediction from a revivalist's repertoire, Josie's tape player coming loud from the van made them jump, wouldn't you know? And, Lucy noticed, the sky had turned the color of Pauline's hair, blue and dusty.

Lucy wished Pauline had come. He'd written in longhand: Let Pauline pick out any one thing she wants from among my belongings. Lucy had spread the home-made will beside her on a hassock, reading Pauline's sentence over and over: Pauline receiving more than the other wives. Did Claire and Josie notice? Pauline, in the time of a sentence and all Jim let flit through his mind as he wrote it, again the bedazzling bride?

Then Josie brought in a wicker basket, setting it on the linoleum, herself on a camp stool, and, as she opened it, Lucy thought it was the kind of sight someone like Patrick-Marion might have concocted in a Korean trench, daydreaming in the rain—the calico lining of the

110

basket, the three etched glasses stuck in little pockets, tiny cubes of sugar in a tiny wicker box also lined in calico, and napkins embroidered with Ralph's last name: how they dressed the twins, initials everywhere. Patrick-Marion came back, but ruined.

Now when Lucy remembers the day, it begins with Claire breaking her glass, after which Lucy steps back in memory in the smallest increments: the curving roads, the new cuts in the old, the farmer's wife, after setting them straight, saying to her boy as she pointed to Josie's van, "They been to Paris-France," and the initial blast of cold upon climbing in, Claire in the middle, a hundred goosebumps dotting her sleeveless arms.

Sliding down from the hassock to sit on the floor by the wicker basket, Claire said, "I'm just beat," and as her head dipped down on one ear, the glass knocked to the floor, split as if in slow motion.

"Don't give it a thought," said Josie, dabbing with a napkin. "Not a thought."

Josie's music clicked off and, from over the rise, they could hear cows being brought to a barn for milking, and, farther off, a dog barking. Heat lay in the cabin like lilies on a moat. Pauline's clomping would have shaken every window.

Lucy noticed then that Claire had fallen asleep, or was pretending, that Josie had brought in a *Vogue* magazine and was reading as she held an ice cube to one cheek. Claire's sleep, Lucy would say now: prelude to ceremony, and Josie's reading: reading. Josie cocked her head this way and that, ice dripping onto the pages.

Sometimes Lucy and Quentin rise early to work in their yard, the home Quentin has made for them, even though Claire will sometimes call and remind Lucy that Nathan is, as Claire says, "on *loan*," if Libby ever wants to come get him.

And sometimes Quentin goes into Nathan's room to gather him from sleep, to take him still dressed in pajamas to sit on his quilt while they dig up the ground for dahlias. Then, if Nathan hasn't fallen asleep again, he will run to the mailman when he hears the dog barking, hold the letters above his head like a prize.

And that was how Lucy got the last letter from Richard. He wrote, "Yours is an acquired aristocracy, *not* an inherent one," which line she let Quentin read although Quentin never met Richard. Then, taking Nathan onto her lap, Lucy sat to think, knowing that Quentin was thinking too as he dug. "At *great* expenditure of will power," Richard had added, signing off permanently with this postscript at the bottom.

Lucy watched Claire sleep, watching for the eyelashes to flutter, noticing the gray tinging Claire's hair, how her anklet was made of *two* chains linked together, a miniature heart dangling from the one of silver. Josie's long fingers turning down pages for future reference, then her humming. Pauline, when invited along, said to Lucy, "I trust you're kidding. Where'd he build this cabin anyway?" Then, "Nevermind, nevermind, you all just drive careful," and, almost inaudibly, "For heaven's sakes."

Josie put down her magazine, wet pages fat and curling. "Are we going to do this job or not?" She wore earrings which tinkled as she moved her head. "I don't know about you two, but I've got people to see and things to do." With her thongs, laced high above her ankles, she nudged Claire's fanny. *"Hey."*

Claire *had* been sleeping; she rolled her head on the floor, and when she sat up, Lucy saw that her eyes were wide, as if she had awakened from dreaming. "Where *are* we?" she asked, and then Lucy almost stooped to comfort her as she often did Nathan, saying, "There, there."

As it turned out—Lucy saying, "It's almost dark, I don't know what you all want to do"—Josie knelt beside Claire, saying in a voice she might have used with the twins, "I'll take you into Spartanburg and treat you to a mo-tel, call Ralph, you can buy the biggest steak they've got; we'll take a dip, and finish this up tomorrow, how's that?"

Lucy stood at the rise and watched Josie speed over the hills, running over, no doubt, an occasional overflow from the scrub-tree forest, startled by her lights. At the Spartanburg outskirts, Claire would get a compact from the pocket of her skirt, put on fresh lipstick, fluff her hair, and sigh.

When Quentin came, she was sitting in the weeds by the mailbox, her back against its post, the box jutting just to Nathan's head. He said, as if she had hurt him, "Get *up*, Momma," and she hugged him, asking, "How's my boy?", noticing that Quentin, as he always did, shook his head to himself, hearing *Momma* and *my*: is it wise? But Quentin had not met Libby and, even, couldn't himself keep from giving Nathan chores and little lessons, night-time stories to help him develop along in life, so what was the use objecting: they *had* him.

Lucy watched Quentin get Nathan's quilt from the trunk of the car, then theirs, the Coleman lantern, and, from the back seat, the box of warm pizza, which they ate on a log Jim had set into a rise by the trees, Quentin saying, "In his fashion, he did get it fixed up around here."

Before they went inside, Quentin looked for a broom in the shed where, Lucy saw, sat the armchair Elizabeth, one of the sisters, had given him. "He was going to re-upholster it," said Lucy. "She was in the State Hospital"—told to Nathan, too, if he wanted to listen. "Out of her mind from, as Papa said, a 'bug' picked up from a traveling preacher. Papa went to see her four times a year, disgusted with her, of course."

Quentin said, "Well . . ." as Lucy imagined she could almost hear Jim say as he rolled his eyes, "What I meant to ask her was, 'Honey, but did he *save* you?' "

Then Quentin showed Nathan how to go around beating on the underpinnings of the house, warning rats and snakes they'd come for the night, Nathan asking, breathless, "Really, really?", holding onto the broom with both hands, broad hands Jim had provided as futurity stakes even if Libby could have cared less: "Well all I know is I'm not used to being *fat*."

113

Inside, Lucy held the lantern above her head, taking Nathan into the bedroom, Quentin behind them, saying, "Careful," and "Well, look at that"—Jim's pictures pinned to the walls, his traveling suits on the back of the door, the bureau almost covered with family pictures, or what they guessed were family since Lucy hadn't met many of them, and, maybe, there were other of his children, rearranged now in the suburbs, with other fathers, who would keep the gas bills paid. Dust was everywhere.

Quentin had made Nathan's bed on the floor by the fireplace where it was cool, had propped open the wood door, even though Lucy had said, "Should we?" before remembering they were so far out no one would ever find them—not even one pane of glass broken in the five years, and the cars' hubcaps still on the rotted tires.

Nathan's tennis shoes sat by the screen, into which Quentin had stuffed an old handkerchief to keep the bugs out. He had made their pallet on the other side of the moonlight which came in around Jim's handkerchief in a semi-circle on the floor. Then Quentin had called to her across the room where she sat on the piano bench.

"What happened to the piano?"

"Sold it, traded it, after he gave Linda *her* piano back, I think."

"Well come here," said Quentin. "Just come on down here," which Lucy thought, was why she was with him—timing tied fast to words so she wouldn't sink.

In the morning, after she had shown Nathan all the pictures stuck here and there in Jim's books, saying, "My Papa" and, "Just some friends of his, I think," and, "Here's a sailboat he had once," and after she had waved them off, she stood by the mailbox to wait.

Then Josie's van was like a moving peony among the trees, silent and softly-colored in the morning haze. The windows were down, music coming from them too loudly as they rounded the last hill.

Josie, parking at the top of the hill, looked, at that moment, exactly as she'd planned—in tennis shorts and shirt, the tennis shoes and ribbed socks white and dazzling. A little bow in the pony tail: picture complete. And no one from that distance would see the tiny

114

eye-lines or know she capped her teeth.

Of Claire, anyone would have seen first the Hawaiian leis of crepe paper dangling around her neck, orange and purple. Josie had opened the back of the van, stacking boxes, Claire brushing past her, swaying down the rise. "You shoulda come," she called. "It was great."

"Her usual sense of taste," said Josie as she walked by, the boxes, Lucy noticed, from a moving company, uniform and clean. She held a ball of string on one finger. "Let's be efficient today," Josie said. "That's all I ask."

So Josie began in the second room; they heard the furniture being moved back and forth, the snip, snip of Josie's scissors, which were the kind that fold, clip onto a key chain. Claire sat on the ledge of the fireplace, her legs spread, the skirt and leis dangling between her knees. "We had, you know, these drinks they make in pineapples and then they brought this little grill to the table, and sticks with meat on them, then sweet and sour chicken. This big hulk of a guy did, what do you call it, the dance where they go under a pole?"

Coming out with a carton in each arm, Josie asked, "Doesn't your sister ever get *out*?"

They listened to the door slam behind Josie, then her van door slamming open.

"So you and them slept here last night?" asked Claire. "Do you know what she did? She got us separate rooms. She only talks to Ralph in private, I gather."

When Josie returned, she stayed in the room with them, beginning with the music in the piano bench, her movements a rhythm, Claire saying nothing then, Lucy stacking pictures into separate piles, for each of them, including Pauline, even if they might not want them. Once Josie had Claire put one finger on the string of a box, to hold it down while she tied the box. "Make you useful," she said, "which *might* lead to culture."

"I hate her," said Claire when Josie went again to the van.

"Don't let her hear you," said Lucy.

"Then you know who I hate worse?" she said, Lucy thinking it was only to herself Claire spoke until she heard Josie at the door and noticed Claire looking up, then around the room at all of Jim's goods. "*Him*."

Josie walked past them, and it was then she began her humming. She hummed through the whole of Claire's recital. It was, Lucy thought later, arranged like a Sears and Roebuck catalogue: children's section, women's, toys, Christmas. It began, "Do you know what he did once?"

Lucy watched her sway on the fireplace ledge, as if to Josie's humming. Or, she would stop, as if to breathe again, beginning another story, which would begin, "Momma *can* confirm this, if it needs confirming. . . ."

At intervals, Josie walked past them, saying above Claire's chant, "Excuse me while I get something accomplished," and, in the short absence of humming—although, if they could have listened, Lucy was sure they would have heard it drift from the yard—in that absence, Claire whimpered between words. Once she put her head down, the leis almost covering her face, and, when she lifted it, the orange and purple of the crepe paper had bled onto her cheeks.

Lucy came to stand beside her, saying in a whisper, "Hush, we all know, but what's the use, now?"

"Use? Use?" said Claire, almost crowing. "Who does she think she *is*?"

"This is excessive," said Josie at the doorway. "I'll finish up. You two walk somewhere!"

It was then that Lucy helped Claire up from the ledge, an arm under both her arms, lifting from the back as if Claire were old. And, like that, they walked down to the little feed store at the foot of the hills.

As they walked, Claire whimpered. Nothing Jim had ever done or left undone was worth, as Lucy saw it, such notice in the objective world, which children never inhabit.

Someday, Lucy thought as they walked, someone will love her, smooth her down, loosen the air, and Claire will lie flat and lovely as a rose.

116

After Lucy had called Quentin to come for them, they drank Cokes by the gas pumps. And when they had driven again to the cabin, Josie had gone, the cabin swept clean and a note tacked to the door: "See you at Christmas, if not Thanksgiving. Got to run."

When they drove Claire home, she said, on getting out of the car, "Get the kid a haircut."

They watched her walk to her door, the hips swaying, the leis dangling from one hand. Nathan leaned forward to ask, "Do I *have* to get a haircut?"

Then, as Quentin turned to Nathan, Lucy ran from the car, calling, "Wait." By the door, to give Claire ballast until some man came to love her, she said, "We won't forgive her."

Claire almost smiled.

"We'll wish Josie *luck*," said Lucy, "instead."

Now, Lucy will sometimes think as she waits, mornings, for nothing, really, that one day she will tell Quentin, always fresh from his labor, what she has promised Claire, after which, she knows, *he* will smile, luck the only *inherent* aristocracy, and he doesn't need it.

Purity

In Hendersonville, North Carolina lived two sets of identical twins, identical twin-wise and set-to-set. Together, in a duck-like line, they walked down Main Street in fair weather, humid weather (when the air is like a florist's cooler but without roses), when it was wet: rain or that salting of sleet they called winter. Any time at all, they walked.

And they liked it, the townspeople. They knew, having been told the obvious, although they couldn't remember by whom, that J.T., Arthur, Bobby, and Little Paul were born of the same mother *and* father.

Her, they enjoyed considering. They never contemplated him, the father, and they couldn't have said why. He seemed wispy, a biological necessity but of no psychological interest, like an egg-dealer, dispensable so long as *somebody* paid. She, however, was like the foreman of some big operation.

First, she'd had the twins exactly nine months apart, as if, having looked at J.T. and Arthur (Arthur being the youngest), she'd felt as ordinary mothers feel about first sons: "Something's missing—he'll (they'll) be lonely!" since one could not see one pair without envisioning a second pair. Had they been triplets, she'd have envisioned three more in her mind's eye, and so on to infinity. Given that spectre, she was, presumably, relieved to have had twins.

And they knew she'd named Little Paul *Little* (it was on the certificate) because he was the youngest of the youngest, and this taught the townspeople that time resides in the subjects over whom it presides.

Little Paul might well have been five *years* younger instead of five minutes for all the ways his face showed he appreciated his mother's last push—the bounty of the nearly-made square of brothers

119

with whom to close up the edifice and, above all, their vast experience preceding him. Little Paul was not only the last side of this house of boys but its roof as well—glass, letting the sun in, which came in the form of Little Paul's smile, he was that appreciative.

Also, the people of Hendersonville, who tended toward broods of eight or ten, suspected the twins of high intelligence, which would prove untrue what they were saying now on cable T.V. talk shows, namely, that if you wanted smart kids you stopped at one.

They imagined that J.T., Arthur, Bobby, and Little Paul had gotten equal distribution, their mother's body an egg basket lined with hay in which each egg had set cushioned, only a string such as holds mittens together linking them. No chance, then, of the yolks running together from some fissure.

It seemed their mother was *purposefully* proving this question of raw I.Q. She let everybody wait, *let* them have their sixth or seventh child with the question unresolved: would it be a mongoloid, a club-foot (which affected the brain), or spineless? It was as if she'd observed the worry ruining the sweet countenance of pregnant women, let those mothers-to-be get courage from Red Cross shoes and high-powered vitamins at the General Nutrition store on West Main. *She'd* publish her results when the air was less febrile.

So, as children, J.T., Arthur, Bobby and Little Paul were totally unremarkable but for the mysteries of the bicameral egg. They said, "Yes, Ma'am" and, "No, Ma'am" and, "We think so, too," and that was about it.

They walked everywhere according to age—steps which knew which had been built first. If you talked to them, it was like going up one step, then another. When you got to the top, there was the plunge down—the boys weren't going to contribute any excess language with which to cushion the fall. "If he says so," J.T. would say, pointing to Arthur, "If he says so," Arthur would say, pointing up, and so on, except that Little Paul wouldn't point beyond himself.

No matter that, among the townspeople, this Janine or that Earl or someone else's Thomas Lee lifted his little flower of a head sooner than normal or bowed out his fat legs trying to walk prematurely, everyone knew you couldn't really tell about I.Q. until a child hit the

120

age of making money. *Then* you'd see if he had wit enough to buy up acreage of mountain leading to Asheville and put a motel into its side.

The townspeople bided their time, a community venture. One thing the boys did do (except no one was sure how to interpret it) was to stay in the same grades together, when by age Bobby and Little Paul should have been behind J.T. and Arthur. It was as if they knew instinctively to hold back.

In high school, the twins were like four houses set down on St. James Place (or, who knows, Park Avenue), ready to cash themselves in on a hotel when the time was propitious.

She, their mother, disappeared when the boys got their first growth of facial hair, with him, the shadowy figure, and the townspeople considered this somehow a grace, the bowing off-stage of the director when the rehearsal's done. Obviously it was no tragedy, Little Paul looking beatific as ever.

Schooling was done with; and now, with them seventeen and eighteen, or when the month was right, eighteen and eighteen, it was time for the show, or the publishing of the data, or (and this was barely considered) the let-down.

The two sets of identical twins were about to break open into a pan, revealing how high the yolks stood.

Before leaving town, their mother had given each of them as an endowment half a cow stored in the Hendersonville Community Food Locker, and no one with half a cow could fail. Moreover, it was said that J.T. got a hind end, Arthur got a hind end, after which one would expect that Bobby and Little Paul would receive front ends. But Bobby got a hind end, Little Paul got a hind end, and the front halves of four cows had been sent to the Parma Sausage Company in Greer. *She* had left town in style.

So, the month the boys turned eighteen and eighteen, it was as if the townspeople settled down in their seats, stilled themselves, and waited in elevated repose.

First, J.T., Arthur, Bobby, and Little Paul began parting their black hair on the left side, using Brill Cream, buying identical black slacks such as Jehovah Witnesses wear, white shirts with long sleeves even in 98-degree weather, and string ties. They bought Wing Tip shoes, traded their white socks for navy blue ones, and carried in the left-hand pockets of their shirts ball point pens with a tiny flashlight on the ends. The women of Hendersonville thought this meant they were about to study for the seminary but the men said, No, they were going to open a four-compartment car wash on the highway to Asheville.

The men, keeping in their mind's eye the picture they had of themselves at eighteen, were more accurate. J.T., one day, let Little Paul go in ahead of the rest of them at the Honda dealership and ask, smiling his smile, for a repair manual of the biggest cycle in the dealership. Little Paul ended up getting the head salesman's only copy, and then J.T. led them all back home, out behind the house, and into the cement block garage. This was like the first act.

While the curtain was down, the townspeople didn't bother to speculate. She, their absent-but-not-forgotten mother, had been by this time so endowed with a reputation for impeccable methods of son-rearing (and not for parenting, the inclusive, because of the father's tendency not to figure in matters) that they relaxed more, feeling the deliciousness of faith, the script.

This decent behavior while awaiting Act II was reinforced by the practical truth, which was that gossip wouldn't have yielded a thing. J.T., Arthur, Bobby, and Little Paul didn't hang around with any of the audience's sons or daughters, their high school teachers had nothing to contribute since the twins had made straight "C's" befitting the truly brilliant, and the boys cut each other's hair. J.T. cut Arthur's hair, Arthur cut Bobby's hair, Bobby cut Little Paul's, and, to compensate for his being the youngest and having, ostensibly, extra vulnerabilities, Little Paul was allowed to cut J.T.'s hair, which grew at precisely the same rate as the others' but seemed to grow faster.

Who cooked? Nobody cooked. They ate at the A & W Root Beer in season, the girls on roller skates having to make wide circles around them as they stood according to age at the window. And in winter they ate at the bowling alley where they didn't bowl but watched the spin of the ball as if studying thermodynamics or something taught at Greenville Tech. No one heard of them having breakfast and it was thought, anyway, that Little Paul got to sleep late.

122

Act II consisted of the unveiling and first performance of the four on motorcycles hand-built, painted, spit-polished, and gassed up by J.T., Arthur, Bobby, and Little Paul.

Since Act II came in scenes, the first performance took place behind the high school on the track field, with only several cars of the townspeople pulling up to the chain link fence around the track. But word spread, then, and it was said that the twins had gotten grease stains and track dirt on their white shirts, and that it was obvious now why they had those ball point pens with flashlights in their pockets.

They peered into the engines with them whenever they had to stop because Little Paul's motorcycle tended to lag. Either they would adjust his or all of theirs, and when they put up their tools and little flashlights, the four motorcycles rode as if on one string connected them all in perfect, unbroken tension.

Scene II of Act II was the 4th of July parade when the twins, J.T. leading, rode down Main Street, perfectly groomed, perfectly-silent, staring straight ahead, all poker-faced, even Little Paul who must have taken instruction. Because of their Wing Tips, some of the women thought they looked like attorneys; because of their string ties, some thought they looked like salesmen demonstrating Cut Anything Choppers at the state fair. But because of the total picture, most thought they looked simply mysterious.

At the end of the parade route where, usually, the state highway patrol directs the floats one way (to the football field) and the less bulky groups another way (to the A & W Root Beer parking lot), the twins, lined up according to age, stood at strict attention in the middle of the "Y."

They held their helmets under their left arms, bowl-side up, staring straight ahead and slightly above the heads of the townspeople who came by to see them off their cycles. The twins received the money, mostly dollar bills and quarters thrown into the helmets, as if it were money not for them but for something apart and above and beyond them.

Ahhhhh, said the people of Hendersonville, finally confirmed in their notion that four, and by extension eight or ten, can be as smart as one. And the women, understanding how the boys planned to make their livelihoods, began to anticipate seeing whom they'd marry—girls from in-town or out, twins or just plain girls?

The mothers with twins, who'd been taught by a Phil Donahue guest not to dress their girls alike since it dampened personality, decided to go ahead and let them wear their cheerleading outfits to the after-game ride-arounds. These mothers (there were two) were thinking of Little Paul and Bobby, the youngest and hence the most probably attracted by pom-poms.

The mothers of girls who sang in the church choir tended to consider J.T. and Arthur. Their girls, about ten of them, suddenly began to wear white blouses and black skirts, patent leather shoes and black grosgrain ribbons tied at the collars of their blouses.

If the pom-pom girls stayed up all Saturday night with the team, riding the streets and converging Sunday morning at Tison's Diner for donuts and ran into the girls getting coffee before singing in the choir, Hendersonville looked like a pep rally for Billy Graham.

But the twins hadn't eyes for the girls. They rode (for free) into town, across it, and back again. On all holidays they rode (for the money which was never spoken of by the givers or the receivers) in parades. And they rode at the end of funeral processions (for free except you asked them to the meal afterwards).

Rick's Laundry, run by two Chinese, volunteered to do their shirts. When in late January, Little Paul had worn out his Wing Tips, Lawson's Bootery provided the shoes; and, inspired, the owner of The Tannery, who used to own a motorcycle, offered to sew doe-skin hanks on the seats and inner calves of the twins' trousers where they'd begun to get shiny. He dyed them black and suddenly J.T., Arthur, Bobby, and Little Paul looked to the mothers more eligible than ever.

And winter frizzled itself away. Spring burst forth with the Spring Blossom Parade (the twins had already been through the Harvest Parade, the Christmas Parade, and the mid-January Sparkle Parade sponsored by the J.C.'s to lift commerce), then the Mother's Day Parade, the Father's Day Parade.

During this prolonged intermission, it was especially assuaging to the townspeople that the boys didn't take their show outside Hendersonville, getting the big-head and disease of avarice. They had

124

been asked, no one doubted. They could have been in a circus, like two-headed ladies and men who starved themselves so they were no higher than 4 feet.

But where *was* Act III?

Did J.T., the manager, sense their restlessness? So slowly!, another year of parades passed, the townspeople pinioned, so to speak, at intermission, eyes ready to receive the (time-wise) sudden and (proportionally) minuscule flash of dark when the stage lights went off, then on, then off, calling them back to their seats. The state they were in, with their pupils already narrowed to perceive the dark, was itself a kind of play. They talked to one another as if suddenly their eyes and mouths were connected, when they would be prepared to hush should a spectacle warrant it.

Later, when it was over, they said, All winter I *thought* something was different!, meaning they had thought everything was the same and they were totally unprepared.

J.T., everyone said, had engineered it—never proven: the St. Patrick's Day parade (trumped up since there wasn't a person of Irish descent in the town) in which J.T. and Arthur looked the same but in which Bobby and Little Paul were huge.

When had Bobby and Little Paul grown so fat? This question went like ripples across the banks of the parade route. And when the twins rode through a second time, which they had never done before, it was like a wave washing over everyone, tidal in proportion.

Bobby and Little Paul were there to show them, J.T. and Arthur providing the contrast, just what stretching does to identical features. No folds (they were young), no indentations (youth again)—just the exact same faces and bodies, each feature, wedge, appendage, grown eight inches farther from its closest component.

That day the money flowed, no quarters ringing the helmets, just green floating in on the shock wave.

What next? the townspeople asked, forgetting that good things come in threes, that culminations can be seen *and* felt, and that greed precedes the buying, not vice versa.

125

Perhaps J.T. spent long slate-nights contemplating the nature of his audience. Perhaps he spoke of his worries to his brothers. Maybe he even fought with Bobby and Little Paul since toward summer they were thin again, looking like the others, without that extra patina of mystery which comes with fat.

What next?

First, Little Paul found himself a girl: Trish.

That's more like it, said the mothers after they'd gotten over the fact that the girl was an import, from Titusville, sent up, it was rumored, by his mother—one of her sister's cousins ten times removed. The mothers of Hendersonville thought now that Bobby, Arthur, and then J.T. would fall in turn like dominoes flipped backwards.

Sometimes the townspeople would see the twins talking on the steps of the Hendersonville Community Food Locker, sure that the boys were discussing when to thaw the four hind quarters for the quadruple wedding feast.

Since Trish had been shipped up, not a whisper from the cement garage had been heard. Everywhere, they walked, Trish closing up the end behind Little Paul, holding his hand, J.T. leading and looking as if he didn't know them. Arthur and Bobby formed a sort of clique in the middle.

Oh, the streets were quiet. But the women went on and made a final push: bleached the girls' blouses and freshened their pom-poms.

It was Fall, the boys were twenty and twenty, and the Halloween parade was scheduled, banners had been strung.

Then J.T. apparently sent off for some other manual since Mr. Peters, the postmaster, said a big package addressed to J.T., Arthur, Bobby, and Little Paul had arrived with the first frost. People drove past the twins' frame house, straining their ears, waving to Trish sitting on the glider. *She* acted as if nothing were afoot but, then, it was said she was an only child, so how bright could she be?

She was tiny, like a doll. It was a wonder J.T. noticed her at all.

That year the merchants were disappointed in the costume sales. It seemed every ten-year-old boy in Hendersonville wanted to wear a white shirt, string tie, black slacks, and his cousin's helmet, as if an outfit would put the twins back on their cycles. The girls under twelve wanted to wear dresses like Trish's—sateen, with ruffles where sleeves should have been, and ballerina slippers.

Or was it their mothers and fathers outfitting them like this? "Don't tell," they might have whispered, thinking if J.T. could send off for something in the mail, they could keep the doors of their parlours closed.

Not once did the townspeople consider that they were trying to help along a phenomenon which they'd never helped along before.

So they lined up on Main Street at 11:00 a.m., everyone appearing normally-attired since the costumes were only for after dark. And they waited: Act IV. What would J.T. have thought of this time?

They'll ride horses, someone said, then someone else reminded the speaker that you couldn't ride a horse in a garage. Another person said they'd roller skate, remembering the boys' long evenings at the bowling alley, watching the spins. Maybe, someone said, J.T. and Arthur will be fat this time, which no one took seriously.

Finally they simply waited. The wait made their feet sore and the cold tinged their fingers.

Then they came: first the band from the VFW Hall, then the blue-and-gold high school band, and the sheriff's car, the mayor's red car, the float of the DAR ladies, then the Junior High Band, followed by five horses with the Junior League members' daughters riding while the Junior League members' husbands held the reins; and the float with one driver pulling a ton of corn cobs on a flat-bed truck. Everyone was bored.

Finally J.T. was sighted—high time.

They looked carefully at his hair, parted on the left side, and at his string tie, and pen-less shirt pocket. Then they looked at Arthur: no change. Then at Bobby: no change, all three with that straight-ahead stare, as if they saw for miles.

Then came Little Paul, looking straight ahead as if he didn't acknowledge that on his left side Trish rode in a side car built onto Little Paul's motorcycle, the kind of side car the Germans used when the war started going bad. And Trish, dressed in a white blouse with a black ribbon dangling from the neck, waved and waved as if nothing were wrong.

127

It made the townspeople laugh.

They had an instant's vision of Little Paul's and Trish's children in little side cars all over Little Paul's cycle, and, when that was crowded, they'd have to build one onto Bobby's cycle, then another, then some onto Arthur's, and so on until even J.T. had one of Little Paul's and Trish's kids stuck on his handlebars.

And the laughing was a let-down.

It rolled through the street like pebbles in a dry creek bed. Even Trish picked it up and began to giggle behind her waving arm. J.T. turned once to stare at her, and J.T. had never before turned his head while on parade.

That day, not only did J.T., Arthur, Bobby, and Little Paul not make any money. They also were directed at the "Y" ending the parade route to turn with the groups heading toward the A & W Root Beer parking lot, just like any other less bulky group.

It was over. Whatever it had been.

In time the boys all got wives, one at a time, who had children (no twins), and they rode in cars like everyone else. They took the hind ends of their cows out of the frozen food locker one at a time, and when they were eaten, ran up a bill at the Piggly Wiggly. She, the mother, was heard of now and then, and they said she acted as if nothing had happened.

The townspeople eventually forgot, except at parades they would feel unaccountably wistful, and blame it on the weather.

One wistful afternoon, while stopped at a railroad crossing, the president of the Ladies Literary Guild, who was also the mayor's wife, began to think. Years had passed, so it was difficult. She thought she'd try to get the Guild to pursue a more liberal admissions policy to its membership. She thought, really, one ought not think badly of people at bowling alleys or on the steps of the communal food locker or on motorcycles.

Renters

There are five people in this family. I stand at the dining room door because my sister is laying out the silver—heavy forks and knives with silver handles. I remember from a dinner conversation that they were the best Royal had for sale that wealthy year of my parents' marriage. Now, as I watch Sara leaning across the table to place our father's setting last, I wonder if she is caught in a memory as I am caught when I set the table—mine of our mother's argument with him over the initials, his, not theirs, on the knife handles.

In the memory, which ruins the setting ceremony, I hear our mother whine, "But Lou, nobody does it that way." She makes the whine sound as innocent as possible (I see her lips working at control), and he answers in his atonal way, "I did." Then our mother hisses, "You think you can take them with you if you ever want to leave." A silence falls because we recognize her truth.

But does she know how unnecessary it is to repeat this accusation? It pervades our house, has little to do with silver, that ownership which no one cares about finally when the arguing really begins. Owning silver, I think, is like me taking grape juice at Communion when I know I am not saved.

Does Sara know what pervades our house? I never ask. We don't talk to one another, so now I watch her as a stranger one grows to know the movements of but never the motivations. The sun catches light in her hair, and I see the mystery of her beauty, obvious only when her head is turned away, not because her features are irregular but because her face says nothing but one final "no." I want to ask, "No, *what?*" because, for me, the particulars matter.

When she turns toward me suddenly and says in the voice of our father, "Shut up," I am shocked, not because I have said nothing but because her fury is pure.

I let go of the other knob, turning away. My sense of shock at her sudden spitting words is permanent, so the tightening and letting go is permanent also. She and I live this way in this house, and we are two of the five.

Outside, he is washing his car while he waits for Mother to finish making dinner. As I sit on the couch waiting, I watch my father and my younger sister playing with the water. Her hair is long and curly, darkened in spots with droplets of water from the hose she turns on my father's soaped fenders. They laugh together, showing good teeth, hers because she is young and his because he visits the dentist regularly although no one else in the family is allowed this expense. I watch them throw back their heads, their mouths wide, and I hear in my mind the cracking sound my mother's jaw makes, like a tapped cave when she opens her mouth that wide. The appraising dentist says it will cost $250 to fix my mother's mouth, so instead she chews tight-lipped and tries not to yawn.

But there will be no real sleepiness in her tonight, only the faked sigh which will signal our bedtime. This is my father's first time home in five months. He and Carolyn are washing off California bugs and the brown spot made, he said, by a Nevada bird. My mother laughed as if what he said could mean anything, and I saw no feathers.

Sara breaks a glass and says, "Shit." Our mother begins singing from behind the swinging door of the kitchen: "Black is the color of my true love's hair," and then it is dinner time.

We wait for him around the oak table which is smooth from our mother's refinishing, exactly like others left behind in other houses, as this one will be left. Behind us sits the bureau that came on the truck with the table, thrown in free. A bra strap hangs out of the top drawer because our mother is not careful with her personal belongings. She uses the bureau for her underclothes because she sleeps on the couch and wants to make this part of the house hers. I lean over to stuff in the strap, but Sara kicks me under the table and I draw back. Her eyes do not tell me why.

We are nervous waiting — Carolyn is hungry — listening together to the sound of water running. I imagine him pushing back the cuticles on his left hand since once I saw in his suitcase a nail pack with a white pencil. He is proud of his big hands and keeps them neat. His hands, like his face, are important to his job, or the prospect of a job. When did he work last? I watch our mother straighten her blouse as she hears the water shut off, and I wonder if she knows. But I cannot ask.

He comes out wearing a clean pair of dress pants and a white shirt with starched French cuffs, holding gold cuff links with red-eyed snakes on the squares. The eyes catch the same light in Sara's hair. The red flecks of reflected light on his china plate make everything in the room appear cheap. It is then, while our mother dishes up chicken pie, that I remember I had stared too at his suitcase lying open in the middle of the living room floor as I waited for dinner. He sniffs the chicken on his plate and leans over to pinch our mother, making her giggle. I begin to realize he's home.

"So," he asks, "how are my girls?"

"I got an 'A' in arithmetic," Carolyn answers, smiling because she is always cheerful, as if nothing touched her. I know this is why we treat her differently. As I watch her smile, I feel mean. I cooperate when we do not tell her how it is here, when Sara and I take her on walks when the fighting begins. And when we agree on lies, I do not let on I feel mean. I will let her be the happy one, but it does not help me. I turn from watching her face.

"And how about you, Sourpuss?" he asks.

"I got all 'A's,'" I answer, as if we were allowed to get anything else. I feel our mother's apprehension as I make a silence by looking down at my plate.

"All 'A's'!" our mother says, too loudly, and our father takes the cue, moves on to Sara, which is a mistake.

"Shut up," she says to him.

"Leave the table this instant," our mother screams. Sara knocks back her chair and walks through the living room, slamming the screen door behind her as she runs off the porch. Watching her go, three of us listening, I imagine, to our memories of all the homecomings, I know: it has begun.

"I try," whines our mother to him and they go on eating. Carolyn does not appear to know what is happening; she eats the way a puppy eats, and is soon gone, grabbing her jump rope from the back of her chair. I stay with them, meaning to catch everything because I think it will do some good.

He talks about California; she asks polite questions. "So," he says after a while, "I told him, 'Hell, no, I wouldn't work for that,' and he said, 'Right, you won't,' so we left it at that. What do they think I am?" he asks.

She eats two more bites of the tossed salad that is his favorite food when it has anchovies in it as it has tonight. "Lou," she says, "I need money to fix the car with." I hold my breath, saying, *No, no, not yet*, but she goes on. "The valves are going. I took it to the dealer in Pickens and he said. . . ."

As he rises and throws on the table the napkin she ironed for him this morning, I see her eyes look startled, but I cannot believe them anymore. If I know about her voice and her eyes, she must know about his. He had warned her the minute she said *need*. I saw his eyes hold and his nostrils flare. She was looking at him.

But our mother gets up martyr-silent and begins carrying the plates back to the kitchen. The door swings and I sit watching them, moving my eyes from one to another with the slowing pace of the door until I get dizzy and leave.

I do not slam the door behind me. But as I pass him, in the living room now, one elbow hitched on the mantle, eyes looking nowhere, I glance at the mantle clock. Dinner has taken fifteen minutes. They are at it.

Outside is mine. I know the trees and the tall weeds and the honeysuckle; I know the dogs, and the gourds I am growing to paint and sell. I know the street lamps with one bulb and those with two, the houses where television sets make a blue glow. But I do not walk to any familiar place now. I go up to Sara and Carolyn because I know

Sara is playing her game again: making Carolyn sit on a hole in the driveway, trying to hatch bird eggs. I step apart, watching Carolyn squat, then move over to look in the hole, then squat again. "How much longer does it take?" she asks.

"They won't hatch, Carolyn," I call, running because Sara is throwing a rock at me. It hits me because she means to hit me. I run crying because of the rock and the homecoming. I hear Carolyn cackling like a chicken and Sara saying, "*Louder.*"

I wait for darkness in the bushes beside the railroad tracks, ignoring our mother's calls as it gets darker. I wave to a train engineer who does not see me. I spit on one finger and rub the finger into the cut the rock made, and I stop crying even the tears that do not count because they are leftovers. I have forgotten now why I was crying and am left feeling nothing but the dampness of the evening through the puffed sleeves of my Sunday dress. I sit holding my knees and looking out into the dark.

The houses close down for the night, and no one comes for me. Finally I get up, saying to myself, as if to make myself rise, "I want a bike for Christmas." As I pass through the driveway I crawl on my hands and knees until I find Carolyn's hole and fill it with gravel. Sara may forget tomorrow and Carolyn does not slow down long enough to remember anything. I try to look through the shades into the living room. No one is there, I imagine, hopeful. But when I open the door, she turns from him, where she is lying close to him on the couch. I watch her remember me. "Oh," she says, "it's bedtime."

It is her room. Sara has drawn an invisible line down the middle as plainly as if it were in red paint. On her side are the two windows, the flowered curtains, the orange crate for books, the radio which she tunes to religious programs, and the closet. I pass quietly through the doorway, going close to my bed, and slip under the covers with my clothes on. She is awake: I know that stillness as well as my own skin because like skin it moves with me.

There is no sound in the room, no loose joints of the twin beds settling into themselves. These are our father's beds, built by him from redwood slabs, so heavy and solid that two men must move them, or my father's hammer tearing them down when we move.

I hold still, wishing I were under my bed, inside my bed. It is the best hiding place in this house. If someone is chasing me during the day, I can slide under my bed, curl into a ball, and hold my breath. No one has discovered how deceptive the light underneath is, that it is a long way back. Whoever is chasing me always thinks to look, moves the bedspread, kneels down to the level of my face, my eyes shut because I have read about the whites of eyes, looks too quickly, and goes away. I sleep then; the chaser forgets.

Time cares for some things. My mother thinks I am just like his whole family, who sleep ten or twelve hours at a time and arrange their lives around the sleep. But I am not like them. I sleep because I can count on their forgetting, going on to something else besides me.

"Are they asleep?" I ask Sara, but of course she doesn't answer. I turn my face into the pillow made of foam, feel the rocking of it as it doesn't hold a place for my head. The foam pillow came after the needle pricks on my back in a doctor's office I remember nothing of but the cool points of pain and the doctor saying, "Try taking away feathers and cats." What, I think now, if I had not slept on a feather pillow and owned a cat? I try to think of the cat that was mine but I cannot remember the house that went with the cat.

Instead of the cat's face, the familiar dream comes, or I am awake and know the dream so well that it makes no distinction now between my waking and my sleeping state. It slips in beyond my control so that in the last instant I can only be glad that the falling part hasn't come first, or the German dreams.

The lady gives a sudden jerk with her foot and says to the girl, "Seriously, I think you could stop banging your foot if you really wanted to. My nerves are shot. Can't you see that?"

"How can she see that?" the man asks. "She isn't like you. So don't expect her to be."

The girl pulls herself up from the floor, arms and legs moving together, leaving her buttocks extended in the air as her appendages scratch the wooden floor. "It's hot," she screams as she suddenly lets her body flop to the floor.

"Christ," the woman moans, watching the girl roll over the dusty boards. She reaches behind her neck and unhooks the clasp of her pearls. She shakes them, and the girl watches the perspiration drop from them. "I'm thirsty," the woman says. "It's this place." She looks around the room. "Too much blue. I've heard blue is supposed to be cooler, but I don't believe it."

The man rolls his eyes at her. "It's not actual. If you were skinnier, it might be actual. Like her. *She* doesn't care."

"I do care, I do care! What don't I care about?" The girl is making dust angels in the floor. She rolls over on her back as she cries out, staring up at the fluorescent light above her head.

"Don't suck your thumb," says the man.

"Let her suck it," the woman says. "She's thirsty, too." She lets the handbag she had been holding between her legs drop to the floor, revealing the garters around which she has rolled her stockings. She leans to get the bag but instead becomes interested in pulling up her stockings. Finally she stops, letting her hands dangle between her legs.

"All that was unnecessary," the man says, and the woman looks surprised to see him facing her.

"Unnecessary!" screams the girl.

"Will they never come?" the man asks.

"Are you asking me?" says the woman, looking at the ceiling.

"God," the man moans. "She's mine, too, you know. I even think I may want her. Yes. I want her."

"Ha!" the woman screams. She smacks her lips together, searching in the cracks of her lips for moisture. "You say that because you think I'm too hot to argue. But they won't keep us long." She leans forward as if cooling her back where the dress sticks to the chair. "We'll be out of here soon." She looks at him, as if wondering if she's lost a part of her thought. "And then, why, I'll be in a different place. So forget it."

I raise my head, struggling out, because now begins the falling part I am learning not to let begin. I turn to the other half of the room. She's not dead, I think. I look at how long her form is under the spread.

It is then I hear him move. I sit up, holding as still as Sara now.

Then the sound: the buckle of his belt hits the living room floor. I touch my dress as if to keep my heart from racing. Then I begin moaning, softly at first. I look to see if Sara moves. I moan louder, holding my stomach now, crying out, getting up, running to the bathroom across the hall, closing on my way the door to Carolyn's room. I throw open the toilet seat and stick my finger down my throat. I hear him say, "God damn."

"No, I'll go see," my mother says, and I listen to her padding down the hall. She switches on the fluorescent light and for a minute we both look blue. I do not look at her for more than a second; I bury my head in my chest, close to the open toilet seat. I cry louder, twist and turn until she comes to feel my head. "Cool," she says.

I moan louder until my cries fill the house. He comes to stand at the doorway in his shorts. "Lou," she warns, and he backs away. While her head is turned toward him, I jump up and run past them, and throw myself onto the floor in front of the couch, drawing up my knees and shutting my eyes.

"*Do* something," he says to her as she follows me, holding out a towel, then putting it down beside me. He begins getting dressed and calls over his shoulder at the front door, "I'm going out."

"Lou," she says, breathless, "wait. . . ." I hear his car door slam over my cries. Turning, she pulls me down the hall as my cries get softer. She tries to lift me into the bathroom but I hold onto the doorframe until she pulls my arms too hard. "*Now* where does it hurt?" she asks. I point to my stomach and look into her face.

Sara comes to stand at the door as our mother pulls from the nail beside the toilet a rubber bag I thought was only hers. She fills it with water and attaches the tube. I begin to crawl across the blue tile until her foot catches my back. As I feel her foot on my back, I am sick. I vomit onto the floor as she pulls down my panties and sticks the black tube into me.

I hear Sara slam the door to our room. My mother leaves me. I crawl through the puddle on the floor, freed, and roll into the hall and rest, listening to water drip onto the floor and to the sound of her car as it races past the bedroom window and over the railroad tracks.

I get up and walk softly to the bedroom where her form is as straight as it had been. I try not to breathe. I slowly take off my wet dress and lie down. Two of us now are straight and stiff in our beds.

Suddenly she says to me a voice I have never heard her use, "It's all right. Someday we'll go some other place, alone."

Then, in silence, I learn the power of words, Sara's aching body having shoved them out alive.

Swannery

"Roosters, what are you projecting?"
Elizabeth Bishop

She doesn't think that Rufus will, again, sit at their table, the love poussette performed over glazed ham. Elizabeth had made them all hold hands for the blessings. Four dinners they got with him, four breakfasts during which to watch, and that will be it, the fact, as she consigns it, coming to Mona as she dusts Elizabeth's straight, short hair from the table tops—broken-off white philters, she supposes, since Rufus had more than once brushed a hand over Elizabeth's head where, Mona knew, a mole grew, watery-pink.

Mona thinks that, one day, Elizabeth will call to say he has died, and, crying that she couldn't attend even the graveside service because of his wife, the cry will furrow into her cheeks and neck. Her eyes will turn grayish, and, below them and the flared nose, the mouth will never again close even for breath.

Mona tells Luigi, "If Daddy thought she talked too much a long, long time ago, he should just see her when Rufus dies," no matter to Mona that Jimmy is weakening faster than Elizabeth, and will go first by such a calculation.

Already Rufus' wife and children, seated at their separate breakfast tables, have looked out their windows, asking, *Who?*, and saying softly to themselves, I *wonder*, and: *When, first, did we begin to share him?* Meaning love, Luigi, regardless they wouldn't in all time be able to picture Elizabeth. But, maybe, in a roomful, under chandeliers, a woman such as Elizabeth *used* to be, twirling, and, on a side chair, Jimmy holding a punch cup. Oh, if they dare daydream long enough, it multiplies.

So Mona doesn't talk to Luigi of whether or not Rufus has,

perhaps, died in the Grand Central on a Friday afternoon, or whether or not it is worth calculating (pure fate and actuary charts) who amongst them all goes first, or who calls whom when the time comes, though Mona has with a sleight of hand managed to get one of Rufus' business cards, phone number in a corner: it *could* be Elizabeth.

No, love to Mona at this time is an ocean's creatures, conglomerate. The fishermen stand on the pier reeling out shrimp bait, when, maybe, what they wanted all along has washed ashore miles down the coastline, puffed but airless. And: maybe not.

After Rufus has died, when Elizabeth visits, Luigi will hear more about Elizabeth's home town than any Mayor up for re-election could tell, albeit Luigi is sick already of how much he will have heard five, ten years before Rufus dies.

Has Luigi ever loved someone he's seen but once, the sudden leap into the secret pool of the eye, silver-white and flapping—this whole miniature life—a shiver implanting itself on his spine? Mona has; not something to talk about—her body carries the sights.

Elizabeth's lipstick is the brightest red, cherry-colored, really, and runs into the mouth-creases, makes a rim on her Carlton's, is sometimes on the collars of her dresses, the coffee cups. When she talks, she holds her head high, chin jutting out as if she were about to pose for a photograph. In her left hand is the Carlton, ash incredibly long, says Luigi in private, until Mona nods to Elizabeth, toward the ash tray, just in time but not always, so, during the four days and nights, Mona is the last to bed, lifting Elizabeth's chair and sweeping the carpet around it.

But that isn't it, says Mona to Luigi, when she is finally resting her head on one arm, once she is in bed and Elizabeth's talking above them in the guest room has stopped. Meaning, Mona explains, what makes her own neck tighten, *her* teeth ache, meaning: What *is* it about Elizabeth's body that she needn't even describe to Luigi, who says, "I know, but I couldn't describe it either. Come here, come here."

So Mona slides to him, because it is not *Luigi's* mother, about

140

whom Mona romances: lovely even laid out! Mona does caution herself with the reminder that she did not *watch* Luigi lean over her, try to puff his breath into her. Still: "I can't sleep," she tells Luigi. "She'll be up and talking at seven."

"Don't *you* talk," said Luigi then. But even when it was over—his swooping, hint of air, feathers, smell of wet feathers, sounds like no human's—Mona slept as if her neck were broken, and dreamed, like that.

Knowing in the dream (as if Elizabeth, when she still held the girls on her knees, had explained everything) that love with Richard ("So long gone, Honey") would *never* have worked, even if, in the dream, it is almost spring, and in Mona's dreaming eye the hill, which she *never* saw above Richard's house, becomes a dotted swiss of buttercups. And when Richard returns, a visitation, the tow-headed boys, who won't have grown, whose hair always is silk and almost fluid with light—those boys will tumble down the yellow padding to the sliding glass doors and lie at his feet, pretending to be dogs.

Which he lifts up, one under each arm. And so, like that, their loosened shoe strings dangling by each side, he will tour the house. He doesn't think to close the glass doors; a leaf-scurrying wind lifts the nylon curtains before them, and, lifting, the curtains display the high-water mark.

And Mona thinks Richard is whistling, an anthem while the boys, still tucked in each arm, hum: this country cleansed and new and regulated. If, really, the tow-headed boys were puppies, they would wear neck chains; they would be immunized, have perfect teeth, pinkest gums, barks low and gentle so that even older ladies would love them, ask their names. Civilized, Mona thinks, every one of us *could* be.

But Richard takes the basement stairs by feel and, looking, scoots the boys back up and out. They roll over and down the little rise, all afternoon, until dusk settles in the trees, until the mill whistle blows, the flowers shred.

Downstairs, where Mona and Richard lived because, she imagines, his books were there, his cape—black—is where he left it, spread on the single bed, though the books had washed to the corners, pages fat and mildewed. The wall telephone dangled. On the cape is still the impression her body made—head, torso, feet, *two* pairs angled, showing he had been atop her when the rain was over, green a proffered odor.

Then Luigi came, hair like a bear's, only the paws uncovered. Lifted her up as Richard slept on. As he carried her up and out, Luigi stooped to lift the boys' wet bodies by the necks, tucked them both under the other arm. And Mona, as the dream was ending, lived in the mountains with Luigi, two boys scratching in the dirt outside.

But they had no boys.

Halfway through Elizabeth's visit, Mona, at the sink while Elizabeth talks, imagines she remembers having let them go play, so they wouldn't have to listen.

And why does Elizabeth talk so about her town? It's where her house is, tiny under the oaks, yard sloping to her door, a whitish willow perfectly centered in the yard's long grass, and, out back, a path the dog made before it died, Elizabeth herself beating down a path under the clothesline when Mona and Lois were kids, before Jimmy left her: when the tossed clothes in the sun were as good as stringing the house with American flags. She stopped to sing sometimes, even though Jimmy hardly lived there, visiting when *he* wanted. Hers, true, by certificate (temporal) and by how deep the ruts where he parked his car (a long, long time ago, Momma).

Across Elizabeth's street is the Immanuel Rest Home for the Aged, to *specify*, says Mona, who had, before Luigi, dreamed over and over of resting, a grandmother somewhere silent in the house to keep her safe as she slept. The Immanuel Rest Home guard keeps an eye on Elizabeth's house at night.

And, too, the town holds the store from whence she buys the frozen packets for one and the tiny airport from which she wherries to meet Rufus until he dies. Where all but Rufus were young once, and, once, probably beautiful. Her talk: of ordinary things, unless someone listens.

"So what's he like?" asks Lois by phone one of the four days, not knowing that Elizabeth would imagine only relatives calling at Mona's house (which is the case), and so Elizabeth stands next to Mona in the kitchen, ready to talk too.

But Mona couldn't, anyway, have said. "How do *I* know?" she says to Lois, who answers that he must be awful. "No, no," says Mona shaking her head at Elizabeth by the sink, who mouths the words W-H-O I-S I-T, "we don't want any," and hangs up, Lois meaner, even, than Mona herself.

Elizabeth, seeing a book on the counter about refinishing furniture, launched into a description of how, really, to do it. Then, as Mona steered her back to where Rufus and Luigi sat by the fire, Elizabeth began to tell Rufus how to restore a trestle table. She supposed he had one to do; but, Mona thought, wouldn't the wife have taken care of it? And, suddenly, Mona envisioned his wife's pale hair, dried with age but prettier than Elizabeth's which he loved to rub. *There* was a gesture to keep—his hand reaching out; and the one sentence, when Luigi had driven Elizabeth to buy Carlton's: "Let's go buy you some early daisies," he'd said. Otherwise, about his war, the Second.

And he had brought them a set of silver-rimmed coasters, unwrapped and in a paper bag, bought on the way from the airport. He had walked around while Elizabeth got her hair fixed; Elizabeth told Mona that. Mona, by request, had had to feel Elizabeth's hair, for shortness, and then it was that she touched the mole, which she hadn't seen in years.

Now the coasters sit in the dish cabinet; she hasn't opened it without looking at them.

"And what privileged *you* to meet him?" asked Lois by phone when they had been long gone.

So Mona reminded Lois that she couldn't both be curious *and* insist they *marry* before she met them, to which Lois, who as far as Mona knew only typed and ate her life away, said, "Huh," slamming down the phone.

She hadn't seen Lois in five years, Elizabeth the one talking about her size, saying you had to go to half-size now if you wanted to send her a thing. Which Mona didn't. "Would you?" she asked Luigi. "Twenty and a half?"

"But I haven't *met* her," he said. How Mona, but for dreams, could forget she hadn't been with Luigi all her life, Richard, *if* she envisioned it, perched somewhere in a tree.

If Lois ever had a man, did he take her to *dinner* first? "Her voice," said Luigi, "is so sweet." And it was. "I used to worry about her," said Elizabeth on the last night. "But I don't find that much time now," winking at Rufus with a toss of her head, and going on about how time goes until a person doesn't know it goes.

Then it was spring at their house, Luigi digging up the yard, Mona stooping now and then to wonder: *would* Luigi miss the two boys she'd never give him though *she* had them, lodged inside. Sometimes even in Mona's waking life they ran across the yard: Richard's boys flying up to sit beside him on a branch, watching, watching, not always at them digging but at the horizon, too, Luigi's and Mona's house behind them, like a rocking ship, too large, she thought, for who would fill the rooms?

Elizabeth did not add to their store of knowledge of Rufus; she'd say by phone, "I'm going—guess where—to Richmond next week," and Mona would add, to herself, "to see Rufus," the stranger. Envisioning again, too, Rufus' wife—a whole history invented, how long the street, how far to the church, how far back the house sat on the lot, and the size of its trees. In her bedroom was a chaise longue, covered in yellow chintz.

When Luigi asked, as he often did, "What are you thinking about?", what could she say?

And his mother, too—who had once brought her a cup of coffee to take to the bath—oh, years they didn't have grown from that gesture, Mona gathering in, Luigi's mother so like him, lovely to watch move, mouth *not* blurring with words.

Mona's flowers: planted with a vengeance, and their house now

144

so orderly that Luigi, she was sure, could barely move, so Mona was ashamed, too.

Before the killing heat set in where Jimmy lived, he sent Mona a copy of his will and this, unexpected, had her imagining the long black-tarred roads he took to town where the man who delivered coal also witnessed signings. "Wise of you," he would have said, praise always one way to order the world.

Still, Mona called the aunts, "Go see," since, of course, Jimmy wouldn't have a telephone. Luigi then had to watch her pace in the kitchen, had in fact helped her remember the aunts' names. Their wild red hair, and eyebrows like Jimmy's, had always made her think of them as swishing underwater; thus, to Mona, they had faces no names could hold.

"Why he's just fine," they said, in turn. "Was eating his greens and tomatoes when we drove up." Which Mona doubted, Elizabeth, all those years pining for a man who ate greens?

Mona and Luigi were to get his land, a place for boys such as Richard's, where the neighbor's cows would let them ride. To Elizabeth *and* to Lois, who said once to Mona that she wouldn't see him *especially* if he were dying: a dollar, spelled out in Jimmy's hand. And to the second wife, the LaVier. "Most beautiful thing he owns," she said to Luigi, "so *she* must have been beautiful, yes?" But Luigi shrugged, watching Mona's hands shake, Mona knowing he watched.

Then, in their natural season, Rufus sent to Mona the bunch of daisies, note written, she thought, by the florist, saying, "Rufus" and "Thank you."

For what?, Mona thought, and replenished his with those Luigi grew, keeping Luigi's in the same blue vase, so it was as if Rufus sent flowers every day, no doubt one of life's impossible items which flashed through his mind on the submarine, long before Elizabeth, Mona, Luigi, or his own kin, however many, strung themselves out on those several American streets.

145

"You didn't hear her story," said Luigi one morning. "I think you were taking a bath, but I thought, 'Surely Rufus has heard this before.'"

"She cried."

Yes, yes, because even as Mona had bathed, she felt weighted, even her arms floating salted. And had Luigi asked—any time—Mona could have said, "Wait," or, as Lois would have, rolled her eyes, "I can't *wait*": Elizabeth's parents, when Elizabeth was ten, climbing out of their car in front of her, then the city bus tossing them sky-high.

And, afterwards, an aunt Mona never met sending Elizabeth off to a boarding school where they didn't have books with enough pages of anything to see her through. No balm of Gilead in words.

For her part, Mona as a child could not decide: did she, in Elizabeth's stead, hate the school librarian?

And Elizabeth talked, them listening (even through the walls, Rufus) because Lois, for one, had said, "*I* won't."

So it was, when Elizabeth called on an otherwise fine spring day, saying, "Rufus died"—two words—Mona knew one feathered eye had risen.

"We have to bring her here to live," Mona said to Luigi, "so she can talk." Love a long crook, when it seems a person's scream might finally lift and fly.

Love, so fright wouldn't make small boys fall out of trees.

Partridges, 1950

It was the hunting season, and the woods behind our house opened paths of sunlight. The ground, padded with decaying leaves, seemed invitational. Even the weather, after the humid days of September, seemed soft, to be calling.

I had planned to go among the hunters since, like every girl raised in the non-aristocratic hollows of the South, I had a vest, a cap, my eyes, trained. Then, suddenly, I ceased going to the fort of twigs I had built there. I felt too old or, more likely, my body, needing to be touched, asserted its own regimen of class: at age twelve I grew cautious. I sometimes thought it was Johnny, deep in the trenches of Korea, teaching me the need for substantial cover.

From the porch, I watched Johnny's father Ralph go hunting alone. Daily he grew thinner and his jowls drooped, like a dog allowed to stalk only what flew, its training strained by the residual thrumming of wild blood on foot, in burrows. His eyes, trying to keep themselves turned skyward for birds said, *I am chastened.* His shuffling body asked why.

Johnny, if he knew what was good for him in Korea, packed himself in behind fallen limbs, wads of leaves. The newspapers called the event a conflict. Would his body understand it was a war?

Ralph meanwhile listened to thickets move almost imperceptibly around him, a harvest of noise—scraping fur, muscle-weight shifting, dense bone growing more dense, preternatural sleep beginning in the burrows. I thought he could sense it all; I imagined he saw each animal wearing a necklace of leaves—amulets. He wanted one for himself, another for Johnny. When he was not dreaming, he asked: *Will* Johnny's eyesight hold?

When Ralph came back from an outing, we wanted to pat his head, ruffle his thinning hair, rub the eyelids over red-veined eyes.

We did not remind him it was truly winter in Korea, every bush frozen into light. After all, we weren't sure, never having been there. But Momma knitted wool socks for Johnny and for any buddies he still had living.

And Momma played Mahler on the phonograph. Sukie, my sister, said it should be Bach, *pure* majesty, and I argued, from habit, I thought.

But remember, Sukie, how Momma once told us—it was a Sunday, we were riding over the railroad tracks beyond church—how Mahler went to Freud once to complain that, in the midst of soaring notes, his mind distracted him with peasant ditties? So I imagined girls in tiered skirts dancing on packed ground outside a cottage in sunlight, stray red leaves sticking to their braids. Mahler conducted from a tree stump. Who needed Bach?

Fear was a bird in Ralph's mouth that fall, held there carelessly, as if from birth his mouth had shaped itself for retrieving. When he held perfectly still, as he did especially on Sundays, standing before the mantle, he seemed sleek in his thinness, as if having lost fur in the thickets. One hand raised, the head stilled—he was listening, over continents and water.

Lying on our beds Sunday afternoons, we considered Ralph's gift to us. It was as if he had taught us Johnny's true situation. And, if Johnny died, it would be accidental. Quick, a turn of the head at the wrong sound; he would be lifted into death's jaws like a wilted bird. During naps, we panted. And I know all this, Sukie, because self-sympathy ran in our veins, we were so young then. Compassion came out panting.

On a wall in the kitchen were stuck picture postcards Poppa had sent from Santa Barbara—the Santa Ynez mountains, the adobes of Canon Perdido Street—and a Chamber of Commerce map with Poppa's radio station circled in red. Some Sundays Momma had spread the map across the empty platters, our useless dog barking by her side at the sound of rattling paper, as if Momma were filling a bag with bones.

Now Ralph spread his map, black on white, not cream-colored with California light as ours was. He had drawn a line across it, like a fence running through pasture, and circled Seoul, saying mail probably went by truck from there. We left Poppa's map on the kitchen wall and, finally, using the same tacks, Ralph thumbed his map over it. "Gotta see it day-to-day, Kiddoes," he said.

"*Me?* A 'Kiddo'?" Momma asked, turning from the stove and smiling, as at Poppa when he visited. Sukie kicked me as water flowed over our hands—"*See?*" For Ralph wasn't related by birth but inherited through Lela. Sukie had her eye on Momma and Ralph. She said Poppa didn't come often enough to "fix her." How often, Sukie, I want to ask now, does a woman have to be "fixed"? Does a body sleep while waiting or prowl in its darkness?

When Johnny was called up, Lela, *sick unto death,* said Momma, *sick unto death,* meaning the body first, the mind agreeing, took a bus, with one suitcase filled with flannel nightgowns, out to Los Angeles, to live with Estelle in Estelle's four rooms near the canning factory.

Calling Momma from the farm during the summer, Ralph had reported that Lela had slept all the way, forgetting even to eat her baby food, and Estelle had said she had to lift Lela off at the station, people staring at, as Estelle said, "one growed woman carrying another growed woman." As an afterthought, Estelle had sent Ralph a post card, asking, "Are all of you crazy?"

Lela wanted to be nearer the side of the world she imagined her son would return from. It may have seemed to her like a race over water—Lela's body held to its slip by the thinnest rope and Johnny's tacking toward her.

"So what could *I* do?" asked Ralph.

For a time, he went on living at the farm, mostly outside, on the land, seeing to the cows and the team of black boys who navigated the cows from the fields at milking time. And I think Ralph spent time moving the salt licks closer to the house. Suddenly, it seemed, I discovered them when we went to check on him. They were a dull yellow from the cows' tongues, the color *they* were, Ralph said. "Johnny, shooting at someone *yellow.* . . ."

When Momma brought Ralph to live in the back room of our house, off the kitchen, Sukie said, "Oh God," sighing the words, as if she were already tired. For days after he unpacked, she only trailed her fingers over the piano keys, listless, sweat beading on the back of her neck, the rest of her dry as August grass.

Later, when school began and Momma brought the junior grades together for the weekly music lesson, I looked across the aisle to see that Sukie wouldn't open her mouth. She kept her eyes closed, her head tilted back on the wooden seat, strands of her yellow hair trailing over it. Her long fingers laced in her lap.

I thought, then, how quiet it must be in our house, Ralph in his room with the door open, the piano in the dining room with its lid shut, and Ralph listening to the faucet drip in the kitchen.

When Momma gave her Saturday violin lessons, Ralph listened at first from the front stoop. He sat smoking, the Camel cupped in his right hand as if to hide it, and I asked him, "Won't you burn your hand that way?" He said it was how Johnny smoked over there. "Can't let them see even a bit of light, Kiddo." Then he shut his eyes as the twins murdered Mendelssohn inside.

Then Ralph moved to the low, upholstered chair without arms by the windows in the dining room. He watched Momma with sun coming over his left shoulder, and he didn't smoke. Blood flowed to his hands, the fingers swelling, reddening, he sat that still. In his overalls he looked like an uncle who had brought his brother's girls for their lesson because something tragic had happened at home which no one would tell them. I almost liked the twins when Ralph sat watching.

"He's thinking of Lela," Momma said. "I can feel it in my back."

Johnny's letters came by way of Rufus, the oldest of Ralph's black men, the one permitted to drive the truck and, Momma said when she took the damp letter from between the quart milk bottles, the dumbest. Johnny's handwriting would seep across the envelope even as she carried it to Ralph before we went to school. Seeing the letters unopened, we thought they could tell us all we wanted to know. Momma drove better on a day of one of Johnny's letters.

But, those evenings, at the supper table, Johnny's words were like pebbles dropped down a bottomless well. Ralph said, "He acts like I'm Lela and can't hear the truth."

150

Momma said, "Well you know boys," beginning, herself, to sigh.

I thought, each time I heard Momma sigh, of how Poppa ran his radio station in climate which was always warm, where girls wore Bermudas any time, even down his street. I imagined, looking sideways at Sukie, she saw what I saw: Poppa's oriental weather girl calling the national weather bureau each morning and reporting, "Sunny and mild." From her smile would come a flare of teeth.

The days grew colder. Ralph had Rufus come over one Saturday and assemble the oil heater Momma stored during summer under the porch. When Ralph stood by the mantle, he had now to stand to one side, where the mirror couldn't reflect the back of his head. The patch of light which previously shone from the bald circle disappeared from the mirror.

Sometimes he put both hands, palms flat, across the top slats of the heater, forgetting as he daydreamed, until his palms were ribbed with heat. Then—he had long given up wearing his overalls and wore now his shiny, black Sunday pants—he hooked his fingers inside his belt, the lattice of welts, I imagined, heating his stomach through his white shirt.

While Sukie practiced piano after the twins had left, their dollars curling on top of the upright, Ralph drove Momma's car to the farm, Momma beside him, me in the back. They leaned on a fence, Momma with the collar of her camel's hair jacket turned up, Ralph in his navy blue sweater that buttoned down the front.

Looking out at the cows, he talked to her, almost a whisper. From the seat of the tractor I watched their heads become circled with red as the sun lowered.

After they finished talking, Ralph stood still, looking across the wavering fields to the horizon. Momma stomped her feet to keep warm. I was sure that when Ralph turned, he couldn't see Momma, saw, instead, two red circles separated by the width of her nose. Maybe I was the only one, then, to remember Poppa's circle on the map, the sunlit streets of Santa Barbara.

When we got back, Momma's dollars would be sticking from the notebook in which she kept stamps and the record of lessons. The piano lid would be down. "It's freezing," Momma would say, Ralph

151

slapping Momma's padded backside and turning her toward the heater. Sukie, from the sofa with her piano score and pencil, would roll her eyes. I want to write to Sukie now, asking: How old was Ralph then? *Old enough,* she would say, words spitting. But Sukie, I would answer, he grew younger with fear than Johnny and younger, we *all* know, than Lela.

Estelle sent a telegram, short, to save money—Estelle's way: *Lela died.* Momma's breath sucked in, one hand found her stomach, the other, holding the telegram, raised across her eyes, as if shading them from glare. "Get him," she said to me and, for the first time, I knocked on Ralph's door.

"It's Lela," I said, and he trotted through the kitchen, past Johnny's map, past the piano and Ralph's armless chair, his arms held close to his sides as if he would run for miles.

When he read the telegram, he said, softly, "Poor Lela, poor Lela," and I noticed that his feet were bare.

Sukie jumped from the sofa. She screamed, "Is that all you got to say, 'Poor Lela'? Is that *it?*" and she ran from the house, sweaterless, the door slamming behind her.

Ralph took the telegram to his room, and I heard his door close quietly. Momma looked into my eyes, hers a searing vacancy, then she followed Sukie outside.

From a window I watched her standing over Sukie, who sat on the Hudson bumper, her legs stiff before her on the gravel. I saw Momma's right hand lift, as if to encompass L.A., Korea, Santa Barbara, all the world. And finally Sukie lifted the hem of her dress to her eyes.

After that, Sukie grew quiet. If she played the piano, she trailed her fingers over the keys, beginning always at the high notes, one arm resting on the left side of the piano, her head resting on the crooked arm, yellow hair draped. We mourned by no song, many notes.

Estelle had Lela cremated; it was the way they did things there. This news came by letter, which asked, too, why Ralph couldn't have flown out.

152

It was Momma who answered Estelle. Did you ever see that letter, Sukie? As if writing to a child, she told Estelle that decency is not always obvious; some water, Momma said, can be vile with disease while looking clear as glass. She wrote, "Ralph loved her purely. He fears for Johnny. Johnny came from her."

On the 15th day of November, Momma began baking the fruitcakes she would send to Poppa, to Estelle, to Johnny if he lasted. The kitchen filled with the odor of cinnamon, nutmeg. Cartons of green and red candied cherries, green and red citron sat like jewels on the counter. Ralph sat on his bed with the door open, a bowl of walnuts in his lap, which now and then he would remember, lifting a walnut, turning it in his fingers, then crushing the shell with pliers he had found in the Hudson trunk.

Momma baked to the sound of his radio tuned to news and gospel songs. She believed all news too old to be worthy and she hated the songs. She called to him once, "You should get your boys to take you to church sometime. See what those songs are *supposed* to sound like. Not watered down, you know?"

"I know," said Ralph. "I *do know.*" Meaning what, his voice flat?

Later she soaked the heavy, rectangular cakes in rum. I remember: Ralph came out of his room, sniffing. He laughed. The sound startled us.

Johnny's letters came, irregularly. We drank less milk. We spread Ralph's map more often across the emptied plates. Before Thanksgiving, because he had given up his walks with his gun, Ralph said, one morning, he would try his hand at getting us a turkey at the Tryon annual shoot. "Can't let myself get rusty and have Johnny ashamed of me when he gets back."

Do the fingers always remember, as the body in water remembers lungs pushing the head above water? The turkeys flew and his polished rifle swept from the crook of his arm, and the turkeys fell. Heavy bodies without wingspan gathering air. "He's on a *roll*," a man called from the bleachers and, for a second, I imagined Ralph curled into a ball, his black suit-coat grown to him, rolling him down a hill, gunfire grazing his fur as he rolled. A breath of air coiled from my mouth. I almost cried out in warning.

On the way home, Rufus and I rode in the back of the pick-up and brought turkeys from the truck bed for some of Rufus's kin living between Tryon and Greer. The turkeys' feet were tied; we slung them over our shoulders, Rufus whistling at his cousins' doors. Ralph watched from the cab of the truck, the engine humming.

We plucked ours by the old pump, Ralph using the hacksaw to sever the head and feet, burying them beneath the first tree of the woods. He shivered. How could we eat now, Ralph and I?

But we ate. Does Sukie remember? The table was clothed in white damask, and Momma's swans of salt, all four of them, sat by the water goblets. We said a blessing, but no one mentioned Lela or Johnny or Estelle or Poppa. No need; they seemed to assemble behind our chairs, changing places behind us as if looking over our shoulders at cards we held, placing bets in whispers. Johnny, I imagined, laughed. I thought I saw his lips curling upwards.

That dinner was the first piece of felt on a picture such as we made in Sunday school. A mauve wedge, the color of roses. The days turned even colder—medium blue, a rectangle, like the fruitcakes. Frost closed light from the windows until, when we looked through them, it seemed the sun was moonlight.

Sukie took a job at Kress's (green and white) for Christmas money, and Poppa's huge box came, filled with oranges, grapefruits, lemons, limes. Our mouths ached, puckering inside. And, for me, he sent a doll of straw, tiny and intricately woven, as if Momma had sent pictures and he could tell I was old, now, for a doll to hold in my arms. Yet we took no actual pictures then.

For Momma he sent a basket woven in Mexico, and for Sukie bottles of nail polish, a different color for each nail. When she ran her fingers over the piano keys, a rainbow arched.

Momma called the florist to ask, in early December, what it would cost to send Estelle a dozen yellow roses and, later, Ralph and I drove in Momma's car to the florist shop where he signed a card, to be mailed inside a larger envelope to a shop in L.A. We sent the cakes; it seemed the whole post office smelled of rum.

154

During our holiday from school, Momma sent the twins away so that even Saturdays were ours, as if, in a frame, we were closed off. We were quiet, secretive, not with excitement of gifts hidden from each other in the house. Now it was habit.

Ralph had Rufus come for him in the truck one Wednesday night when Momma was at choir practice, and I thought he went to hear gospel songs. I imagined Ralph sitting on a bench in the back, the only white man in the room, his thin legs crossed, hands fingering the cloth of his trousers.

For days Momma sat by the oil stove with her feet up on the blue hassock, reading Robert Browning, then letting the book fall to her lap as she slept, little puffs of air seeping through her half-opened lips. Sometimes Ralph stood on the other side of the stove, watching her as she slept.

It is odd that I cannot remember what gifts Sukie gave me on Christmas morning, as if that morning has been permanently over-shadowed by the night before.

Before church on Christmas Eve, Momma gave the dog her package of bones to chew while we were gone. Ralph put on the suit coat which almost matched his pants. Momma pulled from the table arrangement a red carnation to put in his jacket lapel. He kissed her once, on the cheek. Maybe I saw her shiver.

As she conducted the choir, Ralph sat between me and Sukie on the padded bench. He jiggled his right knee until Sukie put out one gloved hand to stop it. He looked up startled, as if he had been sleeping and was suddenly awakened. I expect we all prayed for Johnny.

When the service was over, Momma rushed to gather us together toward the car, her maroon choir robe flung over one arm. Ralph began smiling, and he and Momma whispered together by the driver's side before Momma got in to drive. She let Ralph off on Palmetto Street where all the street lights were broken. "What for?" I asked, and Momma said, "Hush. Don't spoil it for him."

Inside our house, Momma plugged in the tree, lit candles, turned on the oven for reheating the caramel rolls she had made before taking Ralph to look at his cows in the afternoon. Momma poured herself some sherry from the cabinet over the stove and sat with it by the heater. Sukie brought a blanket to the couch. I got the broom with which to pull the dog's bones from beneath the couch, throwing them to her across the rose-patterned rug.

We listened to the clock's humming, then to the chime on the half-hour. I remember turning once to ask Momma about Ralph. She shook her head as my mouth opened and, seeing Sukie's head burrow into the pillows, raised one finger to her lips.

I think now that Rufus must have pushed Ralph up from the yard and over the sill of his bedroom window. I think I remember the sound of their whispering. I think I remember looking up to where Momma sat with her sherry. She must have smiled.

I heard his pillowcase of small boxes thumping behind him through the kitchen. At the doorway to the dining room, he cleared his throat, as if trying out his voice, and Sukie slept on.

I heard him slowly raise the piano lid. With two fingers he began to play a melody from Sukie's favorite piece by Bach, a thread of the whole, looping to her on the couch. It was what he had taught himself while we were at school.

I saw her head move once, then sink again into the pillows. Momma got up and tiptoed to sit beside him at the piano. I imagine it: she leans into his left shoulder and gently taps his hands away. He slides off the bench, he quietly stoops to lift the pillowcase. He winks at Momma. Not a note is missing.

Sukie, no matter, later, when Johnny gets back not dead but paralyzed and Ralph, never having imagined such a thing, sickens, *this* is how we will remember Ralph: Candlelight shines on the red velvet jacket belted over Momma's choir robe. His face is almost covered in a field of cotton.

You rise from the couch as Momma plays louder with all fingers. We see his red-tinged lips break into a smile. A flock of tiny partridges fly from the field of white. They lift, circling your head. Oh! you cry.

And he bows to the flapping of wings and Bach.

The Black Fugatos

"The last leaf that is going to fall has fallen."
Wallace Stevens

Oh Pauline, desire reeling her in. She says to the two girls, "I'm going to Asheville, overnight," thinking, Maybe a *bit* longer. Any snatched time barely enough, her body only partially the silver of scales flipping through water, mouth fly-hooked and airless, and, once-caught, caught. So her teeth itch, too, and her toes splay as if in hot dust, and she puts one hand on the dry hollow between her ribs.

"Sure thing," James would say, sliding over—booth, bed, car or wherever she found him, even on a used car lot selling spinners to uplift the public eye, one of his arms raised while he demonstrated the spinner's sparkling effect in wind. Under that armload of reflected light, she could slip.

"So!" she says brightly, knowing the hue of her voice is wrong when desire is lavender, mauve. Pauline trusts her daughters know not a thing.

"To see Poppa?" asks Josie, her name for him making him ordinary, a man in overalls or a baseball cap turned backwards. Josie's right hand, fingers laced around a silver spoon, stops over her oatmeal bowl. Claire kicks her under the table. What *else* would she go for?

"Bring me something?"—Josie twirling one braid now, looking at Pauline with those eyes so open and clear they would if she were older stop a streetful—cars, donkeys, stormtroopers.

"*I* wouldn't *have* anything," says Claire, to which Pauline nods, patience of someone already halfway to where she is going, reaching out distracted to pat Claire's hand snapping back into its fist. "Well we know *that*, Honey."

"Any-hooooo," says Pauline after a pause, "that's where I'm going. You two'll go to Miss Keane's."

"Oh God," says Claire.

"And you can practice piano there."

"See?" says Josie, looking at Claire or, now, at the back of her head and to the sound she knows is coming, the screen door slamming.

Now they'll have to get Claire from the back yard, car running, its back door hanging open, Pauline tapping on the horn, and Josie saying, "*Make* her come." Then Pauline will have to wrestle, stuff her in the back seat, Pauline's pink blouse sticking to her back in the heat, then Pauline slamming her own door. "Whew!" Pauline will say, as if she's pushed something as indifferent as a wagon up a hill. It will be just *un-godly*—Pauline's word as the trees' pollen floats up behind them, but the word coming out softly as if to herself.

And what will Mrs. Brown think of the scene, her fingers snaking at the shade?

Who cares? "A bracelet with a charm on it?" asks Josie. "Like a, like a tiny bicycle?"

So Pauline nods: *Maybe*, not looking at Josie but over her head because Pauline envisions that he's got her thrown on top of him this time, making her wait, barely wait, with his knowledge of the increments her body takes around him. The tufts of the chenille bedspread make stars on her knees while she laps against him. My God, my God, who *is* he?

Claire knows all this: Pauline asks, Why, otherwise, would she slam the door? Or, if she doesn't, does Claire imagine the sensation of an ocean when a wave hits the torso? When that's not right, oh no, though suddenly the taste of salt films Pauline's tongue.

If we were *dumber*, Pauline thinks, how easy. . . .

"*This* time," Pauline tells Josie, "you'll *walk* to Miss Keane's, together. But not before 6:00 this evening. I'm not paying for her before dark."

And Josie thinks, Oh! This novelty, knowing immediately that she will roller skate, leaving Claire to pant behind her, Claire's gold head a wedge when she whirls on the skates once or twice.

158

How far to Miss Keane's! Past the patch of violets first, then past the Negro girl's house with her twins, then the house of the two old ladies where they must never go, and never know why—one of Pauline's secrets. And way past the Baptist church where Claire uses the piano. On and on it stretches, defined both by sidewalk *and* all the houses of Belton, Josie suddenly imagining herself lifted up—presentiment, is it?—as if to see the span from above, skates dangling heavy as her arms flap.

Years from now Josie will straddle a man she loves, older than herself, locked in himself, because of time, she will think. He had lived as a child on an Ohio farm with his father, then in town with his grandmother. Looking down on him, she will, if only for seconds, remember how Belton looked in her mind's eye from above on that day she sat with Pauline, think she knows just where sat his grandmother's house, the one with the porch reaching around both sides, how he was half-grown then, waiting on a hall bench.

He sees her smile, maybe knows the power of memory which makes the two of them seem to meet, that lie of the ferreting mind while their bodies rock. So he smiles, thinking: Close enough, this'll do, while Josie's halt in memory and this simultaneous smile insures that he lodges always somewhere in her, love taking root.

"Bye, bye, bye," calls Josie, running to the edge of their half of the yard, not one step over into the street, toes hanging off the curbing and curled over it as Pauline's Nash turns the corner. And in the silence the Negro woman begins to sweep her yard, the two oaks rustle.

Pauline, set free, begins to hum to herself, which also she does when he's done what he wants and the hollow of her ribs seems full. Otherwise, why drive so far?

In the house Josie hears the clock tick: here/then, now/then, once/twice, again/again. The bushes scrape the screens; Mrs. Brown's phone rings. Josie sits on the couch. Later she sits with her skates on, their weight pulling her feet down. Momma's clock, she thinks. It was once *her* mother's, and someone else's before that. They all have these

159

things which belong to people who died. The violin under the sofa, the box of music Pauline might play again one day, the Blue Willow china, some chipped, are theirs now because Pauline takes care of it all each time they move. She asks herself, Where is Asheville?

Then she skates through the dining room where Pauline's twin bed almost touches Claire's chair, and into the kitchen. She makes a bologna sandwich, not looking out the kitchen window when she puts the knife in the sink.

Once Claire had a birthday party in the dining room, Pauline taking up her bed and leaving it propped against the back porch rail. Only last December, and the sheet became stiff while the three girls sat with Claire around the table. Claire: the stranger. Then Pauline put everything back as it had been.

Josie closes her eyes, yells, "You better come in, you better"— *Pauline's* voice, but two pouches like time caught in two sacks of breath puff out Josie's cheeks.

So they get to Miss Keane's at 1:00, Claire having trailed behind saying too loudly such things as, "Here I am, a forward having to jump all the time and she won't get me a bra," and, "If he comes back, I'll kill him" (He's coming back, Josie says to herself), and, "*You* had to stand in the street yelling 'Police, fire, help, murder,' you idiot," which makes Josie shiver, redden, skate faster. Pauline, then, when he was visiting: huffing in the dark: "Faster, faster, faster" while the wall shook, and she screamed out once, so high; Josie lifting the bedroom screen, tumbling out, tearing her nightgown to get help. Then Pauline coming out onto the stoop, stooping as if calling a cat—"Come here, Honey, come here," the blue satin housecoat parted at her knees, Josie saying, "What, what?"

When Claire, all along, knew what.

Josie, skating, remembers that once he brought a bag of toys. On the back porch in a dishpan the Dipsy Deep-Sea Diver bobbed up and down in water.

"And now this," Claire calls.

160

"Hi, Lucy," says Claire when Miss Keane opens the door in her navy blue dress—collar white, apron white. Miss Keane looks down at the watch pinned to her dress. Claire goes to the sun room, bangs open the piano lid, and begins to play "The Moonlight Sonata."

"*Miss Keane*," says Miss Keane to Josie while she rolls her eyes toward Claire's curved back and Josie hangs her head, this way of saying *Sorry*—Pauline would approve.

"And we're early," says Josie, "because. . . ."

But there *was* no reason unless Miss Keane had been, only once!, in a smaller house with Pauline, hearing how she walks as if tramping through mud uphill, arms swinging, swish, as if a baby were strapped to her back. Even walking down a street her arms swung out and hit you. She could lift anything. And her height, and the chin jutting out. But no fat, when there was so much to do, even resting, the sigh coming out as if resting were a job. "Let me rest, Honey," until anyone could feel her work at it. Mouth going slack, blue eyes shutting—too blue!— and the voice shut off like a faucet.

Only when she rested, feet up on a sofa, could you see, years later when the black of her hair had seeped to the ends, that she was losing the white hair. So thin you could blow through it.

And now, when her hair was still black she never rested with her head down, feet up. She put her head against the back of the sofa and stuck her feet straight out, suspended. Big feet, with bunions, and narrow but for the jut-out the bunions made. Toe nails painted red.

Only Claire kept her nails short. Even years later, when Claire grew fat, she kept her nails short and spotless. She used a white pencil into middle age. Claire: growing fat as if to let no time in, of music or the men who come with time.

"Well never mind," says Miss Keane. "What you can't help, you can't help."

"We could *help* it," yells Claire over her music, "we just *didn't* help it."

"So be it."

And Josie follows her into the kitchen, the long room with wood cabinets holding light filtered by the trees growing against the panes. On open shelves along a wall sat gallon jars of white paste the children used on weekdays when Miss Keane ran her kindergarten. The room smells of paste.

"I was having my tea," says Miss Keane, nodding toward a cup on the low table, "and I was to take my nap. I expect you'll want tea," a statement, making Josie nod.

"But *she* won't have any, thank you." She spread her hands in her lap where a napkin would be. "And I can draw or read. But I forgot my books. While you sleep, I mean."

"Nap," says Miss Keane. She nods her head toward the sun room. "Are you sure?"

"Oh, she *never....*"

"No, I expect not." She hands Josie a cup so thin it could break if you touched your teeth to the rim. Ridiculous!, Pauline says in her ear, wherever Pauline is now. Where there isn't a cat—Josie watching Miss Keane's cat roll on her back on the windowsill. "Look!"

"You know *her*. How many times have you been here?" Then: "Does she ever stop?"

"Her?" Josie looks around the doorframe, Claire the same, almost like a cat, her back curved over, yellowed by her long hair, and her curved fingers held out. "No, we don't *think* so, me and Momma. We think...."

And what did they think, Pauline only watching Claire walk away each morning to the church, Claire carrying her red satchel hanging from one hand by the frayed strap. Pauline would look up from her book and watch until Claire turned the corner. But that was in summer. During the months of school, they saw her at dark.

"She's good," says Josie. "Miss Conklin told Momma she's good."

"Good?" Miss Keane stirs her tea around and around. "Good? Well, *good*, yes. But...."

Josie waits, to be polite, then tells her about the bracelet she'll get. She watches the cat sleep on the sill, and almost falls asleep with her chin in one hand while Claire plays.

This music: she never gets to hear it unless Pauline takes out the violin, saying, "Let's see, let's see." And too soon: her eyes narrow, when the blue turns gray. She puts up the violin. Time bunched in her fingers where the tremolo should be.

162

Should I, Josie will ask him in the future, having slid off to lie beside him, take *up* the violin?, voice wistful of its own accord, so it almost whispers, neither of them knowing why. He will look into her eyes. Anyone, then, could have sensed his effort, a grace come so far to surface.

"Could *I* sleep," asks Miss Keane. She answers herself by taking Josie's hand and leading her out to the garden, telling her with patience the names of the herbs and what they heal. "Anything," says Miss Keane. "You were drinking herb tea and you didn't know it. But it's important. More people should study it. We *allow* herbs, the Christian Scientists."

She has Josie taste the mint. Josie keeps her hands in the pockets of her dress, which are as deep as her arms reach, and she holds them straight so that when she opens her mouth it's as if only her mouth were capable of moving, like a person on a sick bed or a beach, heated until he can't move.

"She has no discipline," says Miss Keane, stopping on the flagstone path. "You can hear it. Not the notes. Oh, no, they're perfect. We know about things like this since we're trained to it. But inside her. The rest notes don't rest. That's the only way to put it." And she laughs. "Well enough of that." She touches the top of Josie's head, Josie thinking: Pauline wouldn't like that, her hand on my head. Miss Keane presses down. "She won't make it, you know. But there's more to life than one thing, isn't there?" And her hand lifts.

Lucy Keane's hair was white, full, braided, with the braids coiled into a bun. She wore black shoes with laces; ankles thin, almost blue.

After they eat, Claire taking a place at the end of the table opposite Miss Keane, Claire looks up at the clock hung above the windows and she says, "Now, precisely, is when we were *supposed* to come over."

"Ah so," says Miss Keane, also turning to look at the clock.

"And this way, you'll get more money," says Claire, making Josie say, "Claire!" because they could talk about money *in* the house, but never outside it—how Pauline was raising her girls.

"It's all right," says Miss Keane. "Go put on your nightgowns, both of you."

"They're wet," says Claire. "She was in such a hurry to go make love they're wet, in the basket in the back of the car," Claire looking straight over the plates to Miss Keane.

"You hush up," says Josie, because now, she thought, I know.

And Miss Keane slaps both hands on the table, pushing herself back. "Enough!"

So they leave Claire playing the piano and drive to get the nightgowns, not the *wet* ones, says Josie to herself, touching her chest where what she knows now settles. And Josie soon telling Miss Keane that she's parking *her* car in the spot where *he* washes his car when he comes, "sometimes a Cadillac, with the lady on the hood made out of silver, sometimes some other car, like a Packard or a DeSoto." For a brief time, as they get out, Josie imagines herself as Pauline. Shutting the car door, she says, "With him, you just can't tell."

"Indeed," says Miss Keane.

And, inside the house, Miss Keane stands still at the doorway. She walks to the center of the living room. Josie hears her sniff. "Just as I imagined," says Miss Keane.

"Imagined what?"

"And she sleeps in here?" asks Miss Keane, standing now in the dining room. Josie goes to stand with her back against the dresser where the strap of Pauline's pink bra dangles. She looks up at Miss Keane.

Miss Keane slaps her hands together. "Go find them, right now."

At the door as they are about to leave, with the nightgowns bunched in her hands, Josie says, "We should leave a note."

"Whatever for?"

Josie listens to the clock, to Miss Keane's feet shifting on her black shoes in the doorway, a dog barking far away.

"It won't last," says Miss Keane. "You can smell it. Well, how could it?"

164

Near sleep, alone in the room because Claire made a pallet on the sun room floor, Josie says to herself that *someone* would have read the note.

How could Josie leave him, when he was old enough for wisdom and could tell her why? "*I* don't know," he will say, sitting up stiffly in all his nakedness and holding her hands in his. "*You* tell me why. If you can *tell* me. . . ."

But every word Josie thinks of won't do, will never do. So, like that, it was done with.

In her garden, while Claire plays the piano and they wait for Pauline, Miss Keane sits Josie on the stone bench and tells her, "I watch, you know. We're trained to it, as I mentioned. So let me tell you: you'll need to hold on when it falls apart. *They* won't. Your family, so to speak, I'm talking about now."

Josie nods, Miss Keane takes Josie's face in her hands to still it. "*You* get yourself very, *very* quiet. None of this pounding away, you understand. It's—this quiet—like standing back, something deacons do in church before they pass the collection plate, you remember? So don't *you* cry and carry on when the time comes. And I'll give you some mint to take to your mother, how's that?"

And now, Love (equi-distant), Watcher, Tarrier at Old Houses, By-Ways, the Body's Iridescent What-Nots, here is how it happens:

Pauline drives up and toots her horn—won't come in!—so that Josie runs out and sees her puffed face, eyes almost glued shut, and her voice one second before whimpering. Takes the envelope Pauline gives her, with just enough money and not one cent over, so it's short by hours, and runs it back to Miss Keane, Claire saying she'll *walk*.

And Pauline in the car thinking: Surprise lying like shells everywhere or stubs of roots cropping up as you walk along. Which is only the beginning of suffering, the heart getting itself in gear for the real, non-indifferent push up a hill.

Pauline, afterwards, moves them herself to a whole, not by God a half, house, which she kept so clean everything had a place: Pauline's feet at one end of the sofa, head at the other, everything in between forgotten, like bread on a grocery list. Oh it was orderly! The name *James* never once passed her mouth, not then, in the new house.

But that was later, Josie now peering over the back seat, asking, "What, what?" Thinking, Is this *it?*, Miss Keane's hand burning her head.

And, standing like a deacon behind a pew, Josie misses it all but for what her ears pick up: lovely months of wailing (Pauline) and fury (Claire) and his name dropping like a coin in any plate, *James long gone with his trousers on.* A round, only Josie's part missing because she would not loosen up.

They hate her. How *do* you close something down? *They* knew.

Loss, which taught her, late, to love chaos above all: When Claire was thin with music, when Pauline swung herself all over, when he asked, "*You* tell me why," when anything might have happened in the last green time.

Tutelage

It is not the unravelling of her yellow shift.
—Wallace Stevens

When it rained in the morning, Annie's mother, age thirty-five, slept on, as if the rain were permissive, saying, *If you waken now, you'll cry,* for Elizabeth had much about which she might cry. Her relatives agreed: *him,* thinking he might, good-Lord-a-mighty, become a star in Hollywood, when Annie, the daughter, distinctly remembered her father saying you didn't *start* in Hollywood, you started in Ventura and worked *up* to L.A., the outskirts; and then they invited you the rest of the way.

Soon? Annie asked this, to herself, breathless with the word lodged against her breastbone, hers as it turned out, his only approbation, also buried inside her.

And so, for the time being, as Annie remembered her mother saying, the father had set them down apart from the suspicion of the mother's side of the family, on land devoid even of peach groves.

The only car was his, its tires, fat in the dust of the clay road: a sign, a possible beginning, *when* they made imprints, momentary in the hot breeze, and *if* they would again. In desolation of place, what he planned might not get undermined, the mother playing her Risë Stevens and Caruso—luminious Italian, foreign agitations.

There was no toilet in the house, although the fixtures sat boxed in the tiniest of the five rooms, a gallon can of pink paint left in a corner by whoever imagined everything could match. But there were lights and this music. It could be that Elizabeth heard it in sleep, above the sound of rain.

The car, in Annie's memory: its blackness squat against the treeless horizon, holding the odor of cigars and, inside the trunk, pictures of women from magazines, rhinestone straps across their shoulder bones. Still, on his last visit, the father, even with his limp, had lifted Elizabeth slightly off her feet as it seemed the horn still sounded, pinched her fanny, half-carried her into the house, knowing that Annie would sit flipping the dial of the car radio. Then, later, he would be reminded of how Elizabeth really was—wanting if not this, then that, her voice, he could have sworn, a gnat. So of course he drove off again.

Don't ask for anything, Annie wanted to tell Elizabeth, knowing that what you didn't ask for, you got. And, in this way, Annie sided with her father: the relatives might get Elizabeth completely trained: little telephone benches, white milk-glass roosters, washable nylon shirts. And surely that was not *it.*

So, when it rained in the morning and Elizabeth slept on, Annie, age ten and her body looking older, woke with the first spatter, as if sent for, no one, however, to ask later what she learned.

She dresses herself in the aqua toreador pants, a gift from a cousin six times removed and nevertheless close, having seen death in Korea, having wanted, without knowing why, to send a gift especially to Annie. Also, hanging almost to the knees of the shortened pants, is the tee-shirt the father never wore, would not wear—no underclothes at all!—and sneakers, feet sockless. Taking a tomato from the kitchen window, she walks the mile to the aunt and uncle's house—his side of the family—to listen.

Soon her braided hair is damp, the aunt and uncle's half-raised windows glisten, and the white aluminum siding looks washed.

On days when it rains, Coy doesn't go to sell real estate here in the county where mud would encrust his sharkskin suit to the knees and the prospective buyers' hounds would shake the undergrowth. His truck sits on the rise to their house, the dog's house near the truck, the chain leading to it from the miniature tree encrusted in mud.

When Annie goes past the shivering dog, she continues to look at it, to keep him quiet, knowing she must do this, knowing little else of what she is doing.

168

Inside the house, in the room next to what the aunt calls the parlor, where the picture window looks out onto what one day soon would be the New Cut road, the uncle rides the bed. And, inside the bed, the aunt puffs—rivulets of air, at first, as if she were catching up, rising through water, the bed rocking, Annie's breath stopped behind the window's screening, ready inside her for the explosion, the attentuate huffs, the ensuing shock of quiet. Sometimes the aunt and uncle stopped mid-way, began again, the interval a topiary of silence. Annie didn't like this waiting; inside it, anything might happen.

Then, when it was over, Annie walked back slowly, to bring in the bucket of well water or to write a letter to her grandfather on the father's side.

Elizabeth's breathing as she slept was so quiet that, as with a baby or an old person, you had to stand watching the sheet move to know if she were breathing. Always she was.

On mill day (although the mother and the daughter could not seem to remember each week what day it fell on) the aunt and uncle drove down to put two-pound bags of cornmeal and stone-ground wheat flour in Elizabeth's mail box, raising the red flag before they drove off. So Elizabeth did sometimes cook, a flurry of activity, as if she had been thinking and come to a resolution. But often, too, Elizabeth would lift her head from her book toward twilight, telling Annie to go to her aunt's for dinner.

And Annie was shy at their table, not because of her listening to them on the days it rained, since there seemed to be no connection between the sounds and how they were at the table—Coy eating like anybody, then tilting back his chair—but because she knew why she was there and that, when she returned home, there would be no evidence of her mother's having eaten. She would be listening to records in the faded light, head thrown back on the chair, eyes shut, hands clasped in her lap, and her fingers moving almost imperceptibly.

When the cousin who had sent Annie the aqua toreador pants finally made it back in one piece, "or almost," as they said, Elizabeth's relations decided to hold a gathering on the front field of his sister's farm and sent a set of cousins for Elizabeth and Annie.

During the ride, the cousin named Mabel turned to Elizabeth in the back seat to say, "I baked an extra cake so y'all'd have something to bring," and Lois, the other cousin, said, "Well I swan, I did too!" after which Elizabeth said softly, "Thanks, you two modern wonders." Looking past Annie out the car window, she added, "A surfeit of cake," her right hand rhythmically patting Annie's left leg as they drove. Elizabeth was beautiful, the cousins were not, and had not Elizabeth been forsaken, they would not have liked her.

Under the trees, at the other end of the table made of boards across saw horses, Elizabeth's two sisters sat with Elizabeth, their heads close to hers and, Annie could tell, their voices whispering. Sometimes one aunt would touch Elizabeth's fork hand and, once, Elizabeth brushed the blond bangs from her forehead, showing Annie that she was not yet whimpering, no matter they would get it out of her soon.

The smaller cousins asked Annie to go swim with them in the dammed-up creek, but she wouldn't go, saying, "I'd get a cramp," though she'd eaten almost nothing amongst yellow jackets and the clothing heat.

Rufus, who of all his battalion survived, motioned Annie to him. "I brought you something," he whispered. "In the house." And so Annie took his damp hand, feeling that she knew him because of the toreador pants and that she didn't, because of Korea.

"Is that a lavaliere?" she asked, looking up at the dog tag dangling on his tee-shirt.

He stopped to look down at her, holding her still so that he could look at her eyes. "You read too much," he said, then, needlessly, lifted her up at the steps. Annie turned once more to look at her mother, resting now on a folding chair beneath the chinaberry trees, one hand fanning the air.

In his room, the shades were pulled because, Annie thought, the great-uncle had died in the room while Rufus was away, and, because

170

they were curtainless, light edged the windows. Where one shade buckled, a shaft of light streaked across the linoleum. Everything seemed the darker for these shafts of light, and cooler. No one from outside the house had come to say good-bye to the great-uncle; they had said he was too far gone for that. He wouldn't have noticed curtainless windows. Rufus, too, having been away, missed it all. Catching up, he asked such questions as, "Can't none of you *knit*? Back there"—across the imagined ocean, which even his hand, lifting up, knew—"socks was a *luxury*."

"Look," he said, taking a tiny white box from the bureau, on which sat the great-uncle's picture, and tossing the box to Annie as she dangled her feet off the side of the bed. "Scoot over," he added, throwing himself full-length on the chenille cover, boots touching the footboard. Because the bed sat against one wall, Annie sat with her legs crossed and her back cooling against the plaster.

"What is it?" she asked, holding the box unopened in her hands, thinking, One of those mustard seeds in a glass ball.

Rufus took it then, crooking a finger at her until she lay with her head next to his as he held the box between them. They shook—his hands. He had said at the table as he tried to eat corn that they always would, which had made the female cousins shake their heads, click their tongues, as if Rufus had been bad.

"Ready?" he asked, turning to wink at her. And he drew out a tiny gold chain with a star hooked over it, a red stone in its center. She watched it sway. "They said it was real," he said. "Not that I'd believe them."

When he had clasped it behind her neck, or tried, until Annie helped him, she lay back down and felt the lightness of the chain at the hollow of her neck. "I got two things you gave me," she said softly.

"You betcha," he said, and then they lay listening to the sounds outside.

"Show me your toes," Annie said when she'd seen his eyelids move once, thinking then not of his toes but how his lashes curled, hers straight and long, darker even than her father's hair.

While Rufus was untying one boot, he turned to put a finger to his lips. Annie nodded and, walking across the matress on her knees, waited at the foot of the bed for the unlacing. Then Rufus showed her what was left of his toes. She touched the place where the toe nails had been, one hand at her throat.

"Wear it, Sweetie, in good health," Rufus called as the four drove off near twilight.

When the father had not been to visit Elizabeth and Annie for weeks, the grandfather on the father's side brought a peck of tomatoes, another of peaches, and a sack of corn, coming to the door himself, though he shouldn't have, Elizabeth said, he was so slow and stooped over, rubbing a hand over Annie's head, tipping his hat to Elizabeth, saying, "We can't use it all, so you-all help."

"Help," Elizabeth repeated, as if dumb.

Elizabeth waved from the front door screen to the grandmother in the driver's side of the two-tone truck stopped at the mailbox. She was a Holy Roller, which Elizabeth called an infection. But they ate all of the corn, tomatoes, peaches.

Annie began to watch for the grandfather's truck. He was her favorite relative until Rufus came back, this fact her secret from Elizabeth.

"Where *is* he?" Annie asked Elizabeth one afternoon, not sure in her own mind now if she meant her father, the grandfather, or Rufus.

"Making connections," said Elizabeth. "That's where he is." And, hearing her voice then, you wouldn't have known that Elizabeth ever cried.

Then Rufus, having bought a Ford convertible, began to come for Annie, to take her on rides, to buy her packets of Sugar Daddy candy at the store where work on the New Cut road began. Always he had the roof down; Annie's braids swooshed out behind her, Rufus speeding even on the curves, and when they spread the first black tar, going ninety past Coy's picture window, oblivious of it because Coy and Rufus had never met.

"Hang on," Rufus called. And: "They ought to see *this*."

Who? Annie thought. *The battalion,* she answered.

On the first day that it rained after Rufus got the car, he drove up as she was walking home from the aunt's house where Rufus would have assumed, had he known them, that she ate breakfast. "Out for your health?" he called. The tan roof was up and, inside, as he drove slowly for the first time, neither whistling nor sucking his breath, he said, "Rained over there all the time, all the time," until it became a chant, as if he'd forgotten her. The car seemed to Annie much different.

"Let's give it up," he said after a time, and he drove her, without talking, to the farm, where they lay atop his bed, listening to the rain, to Estelle on the party line, to the sound of the radio which sat on the refrigerator.

"What're y'all doing in there?" Estelle called.

"She wants to know what we're doing in here," Rufus said, his voice flat.

But they were doing nothing. After Estelle opened the door once to see them lying flat and still beside one another, with their arms crossed beneath their heads, she closed the door quietly, as if they were sleeping, and didn't bother them again, even turning down the radio, the house becoming as it had been while the great-uncle lived.

One afternoon Rufus raised himself up to ask, "You don't mind?" as he peeled off the white socks and tossed them to the linoleum. Annie shook her head, pretending then to sleep, knowing how his curled toes looked near the footboard and that he would never take her swimming.

In the worst of the August heat Elizabeth stopped cooking altogether and, in turns, Annie and Elizabeth opened cans of Vienna sausages, sardines, potted meat to spread on saltines—all the food the father had put in the cabinets when he brought them to the house, although the girl and the mother hadn't known then that it was his stockpile against his own suspicions of himself. And if they thought it now, neither said. Annie began to lick the contents of the raspberry Kool-Aid packages so that her lips and tongue were tinged, which Rufus said he liked.

He drove her to the clinic in Greer when she got worms, "as you *would,*" said Elizabeth, sick from looking at the circles rising on Annie's arms and legs.

It was on that afternoon, while riding home from the clinic through the Negro section of Greer, that Annie saw on a side street the grandfather's two-tone truck, and her father leaning out its back, selling greens and corn while dressed in his suit coat.

She did not tell Rufus what she'd seen. Looking at Rufus as the wind blew his hair, she thought he might have turned back for nothing more than curiosity. *Even in his tie,* Annie thought as they drove.

When the chain gang working on the New Cut road neared their house, it was Elizabeth who watched. She had gone, a second time, to see if they had mail, and stayed. Annie went to check on her, bringing out saltines with peanut butter, Elizabeth saying, "You can't eat in front of them!"

"You ladies ought to get back on inside," the foreman called to them both, but Elizabeth wouldn't go. All day she watched, not even turning around when Annie called, "They won't sing, I bet you." Elizabeth finally sat with her back against the post of the mailbox. The sound of the picks and the foreman calling to the men, and the barking dog running in circles around even Elizabeth became almost like a movie Annie watched from the chair set behind the screen.

Yet what could Annie ask Elizabeth of it, everyone having seen Elizabeth through one long day like that?

Lying by Rufus, Annie asked of the men on the gang, "What did they *do?*"

Turning to her, he flipped the collar of her blouse. "No more than the rest of us," he said.

174

"Not *me*."

"*Most* of us then." And he ran one finger up and down her nose as he hummed.

Of course the girl and the mother would one day get out, go someplace special, as Elizabeth put it, to eat fresh figs and stop being the pity, sopped up like milk and cornbread.

The father would get to Ventura, but alone.

And when, years later, Annie would drive herself by the little house, as if it were what she wanted to know, there would be no way to tell if it were ever finished inside, so covered in scrub, the withy roots of pine. Who in the family owned it now, who would not sell?

"He hasn't *got* a plan," said Elizabeth, awake one morning when it was raining but as still in the bed as if she slept.

And would the father ever have returned otherwise? — the grand-father near death, asking for Annie, and the father driving all the way up to the stoop, a bag of groceries for Elizabeth, new shoes for Annie, which she was to put on in the car because there wasn't much time.

"This is no joke," he said to Elizabeth, who answered, "I don't ex-pect it is."

The shoes were too small, and so their buckles dangled, made sounds like tiny bells on the patent leather.

Others from the family were already there, hurry, hurry, the father's left hand tapping on the dash: she should have come, she should have come.

So the grandfather and Annie would not, after all, have time for the walk out to his blackberry patch, where he would have stooped to tell her that the father would adjust himself in time, come home like a cow at milking.

Instead, they parked along the creekside, weaving through the cars of the children, stuffed animals sitting on the dashboards and ledges in the back. The father lifted Annie up where the creek crossed the road and, in a set of hops, crossed the yard to the house.

By the door, he set her down. The door stood open, room filled with flies, the bed, the sound of babies.

"Well praise God," they said. "You was the only one hadn't come. He's slipping."

"That's what they say," said the grandfather from the pile of covers around him, laughing once so that Annie thought he would get up again, even without his teeth.

But he did not get up again, though for years Annie dreamed that he sat between them as she and Rufus drove the road to Greer, suspecting, even, as she woke, that others filled the back seat, half-standing because the roof was down.

No: toward morning, waking even those who slept in their chairs, he lifted himself on his pillows one last time, to cry, "Even going through it, no one knows how to die."

And this, by him one last time before they moved away, Annie told Rufus, as if, while her body learned what it might have done, he could cry out too.

Printed June 1987 in Santa Barbara & Ann Arbor
for the Black Sparrow Press by Graham Mackintosh &
Edwards Brothers Inc. Design by Barbara Martin. This
edition is published in paper wrappers; there are 250
cloth trade copies; 150 hardcover copies have been
numbered & signed by the author; & 26 lettered copies
have been handbound in boards by Earle Gray & are
signed by Eve Shelnutt.

Photo: Jim Judkis

Eve Shelnutt, an Associate Professor teaching in the M.F.A. Writing Program at the University of Pittsburgh, was born in Spartanburg, South Carolina. She received her B.A. degree from the University of Cincinnati and her M.F.A. from the University of North Carolina at Greensboro, where she studied with Fred Chappell. Her first short story won the Mademoiselle Fiction Award and, since then, she has published stories in many journals and anthologies, including *O. Henry Prize Collection, Stories of the Modern South, Stories for the Eighties: A Ploughshares Reader, Mother Jones, Prairie Schooner,* and the *Virginia Quarterly Review.* In 1983 she published her first collection of poetry (*Air and Salt*, Carnegie Mellon Press); her second collection of poetry, *Recital in a Private Home,* will be published by Carnegie Mellon Press this year. *The Love Child* (Black Sparrow, 1979), Eve Shelnutt's first collection of stories, was awarded the Great Lakes Fiction Award in 1980, and her second story collection (*The Formal Voice*, Black Sparrow, 1982), was awarded the Winthrop College Merit Award in Fiction in 1983. She is currently working on a novel and short stories.